A JOHN TAYLOR NOVEL

TRAVIS STARNES

Signup to get free previews of upcoming books before they're released at

http://tstarnes.com/preview-notification-newsletter/

Contents

Chapter 1

Mexico City, Mexico

Taylor stepped through the glass doors, positioning himself on the girl's right side while Lopez mirrored him on her left. It was not hard to know who she was, even at a glance. Her father might have been a diplomat now, but he'd been in the news for years before he'd been tapped by the Foreign Office for this position.

Normally, a diplomat's family wouldn't be a major target, but the man was filthy rich and had questionable business contacts stretching back years. That, and his wife was from Mexico, which explained why his daughter, while she had his features, had her mother's complexion. Taken together, there had been credible threats on his and his family's lives while in country.

Normally, Taylor wouldn't have worked for someone like him, having a distaste for his type, but she was a seventeen-year-old girl, and while the British government might protect him, she was on her own.

Besides, the company was still new and this job was bringing in a lot of money.

The street was busy, although not packed. Office workers heading for late lunches, vendors hawking newspapers and cigarettes, the usual urban flow that made threat assessment both easier and harder. Easier because disruptions stood out. Harder because there were so many places to hide.

Taylor kept his right hand just inside his jacket, resting on the butt of his weapon as his eyes moved over the crowd, watching pedestrians walking, taxis jockeying for position against delivery trucks.

None of that was what Taylor's eyes locked on.

Across the four lanes of traffic, two men leaned against a dented sedan, wearing cheap suits that didn't fit right in the shoulders and had a lot of room inside to keep something hidden.

They weren't talking to each other. They weren't smoking. They were just watching the entrance to the office building. Further down, near a newsstand plastered with football headlines, stood another pair, also staring hard at the door. Not looking at phones, not reading newspapers.

Just watching.

Taylor glanced at Lopez.

"I see them," he said.

"Isabella, just keep walking, but when I give you the signal, I want you to run with Lopez to the car."

"Wait, is it ..." she said, her steps faltering.

"No. Keep walking. Don't worry. You'll be safe. Just stay with Lopez."

She nodded, looking terrified.

The two men across the street pushed off the sedan. It was well done. No sudden movement. No rush. It was very professional, the four men moving from two directions, their paths designed to intersect with Taylor's group just before they reached the safety of the Suburban.

The lead attacker was built like a bouncer, thick through the shoulders with arms that strained against his cheap suit jacket. He reached for Isabella with both hands extended, fingers spread wide to grab her upper arms.

His partner, smaller but with a kind of grace, stepped directly into Taylor's path. Not reaching for a weapon yet, just using his body as a human wall while his partner secured the target. The man's eyes were already tracking past Taylor, watching for Lopez.

Taylor wasn't going to let them set the terms.

He suddenly burst into motion, pushing the girl hard into Lopez, putting his full weight into it.

"Go! Now!"

Lopez was ready and caught her, wrapping one arm around her waist so she didn't stumble while his other hand went to his weapon. He didn't question or hesitate, just turned, practically picking her up as he ran her toward the SUV, using his body to shield her from the converging attackers.

Taylor used the momentum from his shove to launch himself forward, closing the distance with the man blocking him. Their approach might have been professional, but they weren't as good as they thought they were because he caught them completely off guard.

Taylor's right hand came up holding his sidearm, but instead of firing, he drove the butt of the pistol into the man's throat, the strike crushing the man's larynx with a wet crunch.

The attacker's hands went to his neck as he staggered backward, gasping for air that wouldn't come. His knees buckled, and he dropped to the sidewalk, making choking sounds that were lost in the street noise.

Taylor ignored him.

The big man who'd been reaching for Isabella had to pull up short to avoid tripping over his falling partner. That split-second hesitation broke his momentum, gave him something else to think about besides grabbing the girl.

After striking the first man, Taylor brought up his gun and put two rounds center mass of the second man, just as the big man's hand started moving toward the inside of his jacket. The sharp gunshot cracks stopped nearly everyone around them for a moment as violence suddenly erupted in their midst.

The big man's forward motion stopped like he'd hit an invisible wall. A confused expression crossed his face as he looked down at the spreading red stains on his white shirt. Then his legs gave out, and he crumpled to the pavement.

The moment of surprise passed, and pedestrians started screaming, dropping things and running in every direction as the world exploded into chaos.

Lopez had Isabella at the SUV, yanking the rear door open and practically throwing her inside. She hit the seat hard, her knee banging against the center console as Lopez shoved her down below the window line. He slammed the door and dove for the driver's seat.

The two flanking attackers saw their plan falling apart. They'd been counting on a quick, quiet grab. Now they had two men down, their target was in an armored vehicle, and witnesses were running in every direction. They went for their weapons, no longer concerned about keeping things quiet.

The one nearest the newsstand got his pistol out first, a compact semi-automatic that he brought up in a two-handed grip. He fired three rounds at the SUV's driver-side window as Lopez cranked the engine. The bullets sparked off the bulletproof glass, leaving spiderweb cracks but not penetrating.

His partner took cover behind a concrete planter filled with decorative palms, leaning out to fire at Taylor. The rounds zipped past, one close enough that Taylor felt the pressure wave against his cheek. He dropped behind a stone pillar that supported the building's entrance canopy, chips of concrete raining down as bullets hammered the opposite side.

Lopez stomped on the accelerator while throwing the vehicle into drive. The SUV's tires screamed against the pavement, laying down black rubber as the vehicle lurched forward. He cranked the wheel hard left, sideswiping a parked Toyota with a grinding screech of metal on metal.

More rounds slammed into the SUV's armor plating as the SUV took off, weaving between parked cars as he fought to build speed. A bullet punched through the rear window's upper corner where the armor was thinnest, showering the interior with glass fragments.

Taylor couldn't return fire while he was pinned down behind the pillar. Every time he shifted position, the attacker behind the planter would send another burst his way. But he could hear the other shooter still engaging the SUV, trying to disable it before it could escape. That was the immediate threat.

He broke from cover, not away from the gunfire but toward it, sprinting for a white delivery van parked at the curb. Rounds cracked behind him, one tugging at his jacket as it passed through the fabric without hitting flesh. He slid behind the van's front wheel, using the engine block for protection.

From this angle, he had a clear line of sight to the attacker shooting at Lopez. The man was focused entirely on the SUV, tracking it with his weapon as it weaved through traffic. He never saw Taylor lean around the van's front bumper.

Taylor fired three rounds. The first caught the attacker in the right thigh, spinning him partially around. The second and third hit him in the side as he turned, punching through ribs and vital organs. The man's pistol clattered across the sidewalk as he collapsed, clutching at his leg while blood pooled beneath him.

Lopez made the corner at the end of the block, the SUV's rear end sliding wide as he fought to maintain control through the turn. The vehicle disappeared from view, though Taylor could still hear its engine roaring as Lopez accelerated down the next street.

At least the girl was safe.

The remaining attacker behind the planter had stopped firing, probably reloading. Taylor could see the man's shoulder and part of his head visible around the concrete edge. The angle wasn't perfect, but it would have to do.

He pushed up from behind the van and started running, not directly at the attacker but toward a sedan parked three spaces down. The gunman popped up from behind the planter, swinging his weapon to track Taylor's movement. Muzzle flashes blinked as he fired, bullets punching through the sedan's windows, creating a cascade of breaking glass.

Taylor dove behind the car, feeling the impacts through the vehicle's frame as rounds slammed into the opposite side. He rolled to his left, coming up at the rear wheel where he had an angle past the trunk.

The attacker was still focused on where Taylor had gone to ground, firing at the sedan's midsection. He never registered that Taylor had shifted position until it was too late.

Taylor steadied his weapon against the car's trunk and fired once. The round caught the attacker just below his right eye, snapping his head back in a spray of blood and bone. The man dropped straight down behind the planter, his weapon falling from nerveless fingers.

Sudden silence filled the street, broken only by distant screaming and the wail of approaching sirens. Taylor swept his weapon across the scene, checking to see if there were more threats, but other than screaming bystanders, all appeared to be calm.

None of the men were moving. The one he'd struck in the throat had stopped making noise entirely, his face purple and eyes bulging. The big man lay in an expanding pool of blood. The one he'd shot in the leg and side was unconscious or dead from blood loss. The last one behind the planter wasn't getting up again.

Now he just had to deal with the cops.

Washington, D.C.

Taylor cleared customs at Dulles International Airport and stepped into the arrivals area, his single duffel bag slung over his shoulder. He was at least well-rested. Being able to sleep anywhere was a skill he'd picked up early in the service, and an airplane was as good as a four-star hotel compared to some of the places he'd lain down his head.

He hadn't stayed in Mexico long. They might have let him off the hook for the bodies, but they'd made it clear it was in his best interest to be on the other side of the border. Taylor didn't make them ask twice.

Lopez could close out the rest of their contract, now that the ambassador believed them that Mexico wasn't particularly safe for Isabella.

He did miss being with the FBI, though. Going through customs was for suckers.

What he didn't miss was getting through security and seeing Whitaker standing on the other side near the security barrier holding Grace's small hand, while Kara waited beside them with her arms crossed.

Grace spotted him and immediately started tugging toward him, her small legs pumping as she babbled excitedly. "Da-da! Da-da!"

Taylor shifted his bag as Grace broke free from Whitaker's grip and toddled toward him with her arms outstretched. He scooped her up with one arm as she reached him, and Grace wrapped her small arms around his neck.

"Well, look who actually made it out of Mexico," Whitaker said, following their daughter to him.

"I did fine," Taylor said.

"I know. Lopez called me with updates," Whitaker said, moving in with a warm hug that encompassed both Taylor and Grace.

"So I guess everything didn't go like you planned?" Kara asked, waiting for her turn to hug Taylor.

When Whitaker reached to take Grace back, Taylor waved her off. The energetic toddler was chattering happily and patting his face with her small hands.

"Seriously, though, I wasn't entirely sure you'd be released without complications after I heard what happened," Whitaker continued. "Four bodies in downtown Mexico City?"

Grace squirmed in Taylor's arms, wanting to explore, but settled when Taylor gently bounced her. "Only 'cause they tried to grab our protectee. We were just doing our job."

"Thankfully, they believed you. Still, you should stay away from Mexico for a while. No one down there is happy with you."

"Tell them to take a number."

Whitaker laughed. "Well, not everyone. I hear the Pemberton family is extremely grateful. And from what Lopez says, the news coverage down there has been overwhelmingly positive about your actions."

"They should be," Taylor said. "Those four kidnappers were professionals who came prepared for violence. I tried to tell him to leave his family at home, but he wouldn't listen. Anyway, job's done. Let's go home."

The group started walking toward the parking garage while Grace continued her happy babbling, occasionally pulling at his ear or trying to grab his nose.

"So what happened here while I was away?" Taylor asked as they moved through the terminal. "How's school?"

"It's okay. I'm keeping my grades up, but if I'm telling the truth, I'm ready to get out and just do something else. I'm getting a little bored with school."

"Bored or not, you need it if you don't want to end up like me, a misspent youth in the service."

"I don't know, that doesn't sound so bad," she said.

"No, you're better than that," Whitaker said.

"You don't have to make it sound like that," he said, not that he disagreed with her. "She could do a lot worse. What about you? Any interesting cases while I was gone?"

"A few. Working on a multi-agency task force investigating human trafficking networks that involves coordination with international law enforcement agencies. It's a good assignment."

They reached the elevator bank leading to the parking garage. Grace had started to get heavy in Taylor's arms, but she seemed content to stay there for now, occasionally making sounds that might have been attempts at words.

They got out of the elevator and Whitaker led them to her SUV sitting in one of the reserved spots for police vehicles. Another benefit he missed from working with the FBI.

Of course, there were a lot of things he didn't miss.

Whitaker unlocked the SUV and Taylor dropped his duffel bag into the back, settled into the passenger seat and handed Grace back to Kara. The toddler protested slightly, but settled down as Kara put her in her car seat and buckled her in.

They were barely on the freeway after leaving the airport when Taylor's phone rang. Whitaker gave him a look, and he rolled his eyes. Since he'd gone back to working on the private side, she'd made more than one comment about questionable clients.

She'd even warned him to avoid the Mexico City job.

Taylor pulled his phone from his jacket pocket and checked the display. Milly Breyer. That gave him to pause. She was the daughter of one of his mentors from his first tour, but they hadn't talked in over a year. The last time they'd spoken was probably Christmas before last, when Roy, her dad, had been a little drunk and reminiscing.

"Hey, Milly," he said, pressing the phone to his ear. "How's everything? How's your dad?"

The pause on the other end was long enough to be concerning.

"Milly?"

Whitaker glanced over at him, hearing the concern in Taylor's voice, easing off the accelerator slightly, letting the SUV fall back from the car ahead.

"Taylor, I ..." She finally said, her words shaky. "Something's happened."

"What? What's happened?"

The question hung in the air. Through the phone, Taylor could hear Milly trying to compose herself, the sound of someone fighting back tears and losing the battle.

"It's Dad," she finally managed. "He's dead, Taylor. My father is dead."

The words hit Taylor like a physical blow. It seemed unbelievable. Sergeant First Class Roy Breyer was made of iron. Hardest goddamn son of a bitch he'd ever met, took a kid right out of boot and turned him into someone worth something.

Taylor would have never made it through Ranger School and Q Course without him.

"When? When did it happen?"

Whitaker had moved into the right lane now, slowing their speed.

"Three days ago," Milly's voice cracked. "But I didn't even know until yesterday. Can you believe that? My own father dies, and nobody bothers to tell me for a whole day."

Roy Breyer had been sixty-eight, maybe sixty-nine now. Old for a former soldier, but not ancient. And in good health the last time he heard.

"How did you find out?"

"I called him like I do every Sunday morning. When he didn't answer, I figured he was out working in his garden or something. You know how he gets when he's focused on a project." Milly let out a bitter laugh. "I went by the house the next day, it was locked up and Dad was nowhere in sight. Dad never went anywhere without letting me know, so I called the sheriff's office Friday morning, just to report him missing. That's when Deputy Ward told me Dad was gone."

Whitaker had found an opening in the traffic and moved completely to the right lane, preparing to take the next exit. Taylor gave her a nod.

"Did he say what happened?"

"No. That's what's bothering me. He would only say that Dad was dead, and I needed to talk to Doctor Henley about getting the body released. Like he was talking about picking up dry cleaning instead of my father."

Unusual. Even the FBI would normally say something, or at least say they couldn't say because it was an ongoing investigation. Locals tended to be a lot more chatty.

"Did you talk to the doctor?"

"I've been trying to talk to him for two days now. Every time I call, he gives me the same runaround. Says he needs more time, says there are complications with the investigation. Investigation of what? Nobody will tell me anything. Taylor, nobody will tell me how my father died, nobody will tell me when I can bury him. I can't even plan a funeral because I don't know when they'll release his body."

Whitaker had taken the exit now, pulling into a gas station parking lot. She put the SUV in park and turned to face Taylor fully, watching but not saying anything.

"I get the feeling you think it's more than something natural?"

"I don't know what to think anymore. Dad was fine the last time I saw him, and that was only a week ago. He was complaining about his knees, but hell, Taylor, he's been complaining about his knees for twenty years. Other than that, he seemed like himself."

"Milly, I need you to think carefully about this. Was your father involved in anything unusual lately? Any problems with neighbors, any financial issues, anything at all that might have attracted attention?"

"No, nothing like that. Dad kept to himself mostly, same as always. Tended his garden, read his military history books, drove down to the VFW for their Friday night fish fry. Taylor, I need your help."

"I can be there tomorrow afternoon," he said, looking at Whitaker, who gave him a little nod.

"Taylor, I ... thank you."

"Just sit tight."

Chapter 2

Glacier Falls, Minnesota

Taylor drove into Glacier Falls just after noon. The small Minnesota town, tucked away in a valley surrounded by snow-dusted hills, looked like a painting someone had forgotten to finish. The snow had already melted off the lowlands, but the air was still cool. Much cooler than it had been in DC or Mexico.

Main Street consisted of a few weathered buildings, a hardware store, post office, two bars, and a diner with a blinking "OPEN" sign. He parked his rental car in front of the narrow building with a neon coffee cup in the window and a sign that used to read Mary's but now said M&J's with the ampersand painted in by hand. The lunchtime crowd had thinned.

The bell above the door jingled as Taylor stepped inside. Warmth hit him, along with the smell of coffee and fried foods. A handful of locals occupied booths and counter seats, most of them turning to study the newcomer before returning to their conversations.

Small towns.

Milly had a booth near the window. She was in her late twenties now, maybe early thirties, hair darker than he remembered. Her eyes found him, ran over him once, then softened.

"You look the same," she said as he stopped next to her booth.

"Bad news for mirrors," Taylor said.

She stood and reached out, hugging him like she was still that little girl her father would bring around. She felt tight through the coat, muscles coiled, and he guessed she hadn't slept. She sat again as he slid onto the bench across from her.

"I'm so sorry to hear about your dad."

"Thanks for coming," she said, giving him a sad smile. "I didn't know who else to call."

"Your dad would've done the same for me."

A waitress approached, coffee pot in hand. "Coffee?"

"Please," Taylor said.

She filled his cup and topped off Milly's. "Know what you want to eat?"

"Just the coffee," Taylor said.

The waitress nodded and walked away. Taylor took a sip of his coffee, black and strong enough to dissolve a spoon.

"So tell me what happened," he said.

Milly wrapped her hands around her mug. "It's just like I told you on the phone; I called Dad Sunday morning, like I usually do, and he didn't answer. After he didn't answer that night, I got worried and drove up here and he was nowhere to be found. I found out from the deputy that he was dead, but no one would tell me anything about how he died, and the doctor won't release his body."

"And they still won't tell you what happened?"

"That's the thing, they have. Sort of. After I called you yesterday, Doctor Henley phoned me out of the blue and said they had finished part of their investigation and Dad's death was ruled an accident, but he couldn't say what the accident was, where it happened, or anything." Milly shook her head. "And he still won't release the body or let me see him, just said that I can pick up the death certificate."

"He just called?"

"Yes."

"Did you tell them you called someone?"

"No, why?"

"Nothing, just thinking."

"The thing is, you know Dad," Milly continued. "He survived thirty years in service and they expect me to believe he just, what? Fell? Bumped his head? Tripped?"

"People have accidents," Taylor said.

"Maybe, but they don't hold someone's body for an accident. Also, I know I said he was the same as always, but that's not quite true. I think Dad was acting strange the last few times I talked to him on the phone. I'd kind of written it off as my imagination but, with all this ..."

"Strange how?"

"Distracted, I guess. Secretive. He wouldn't tell me what he was up to, just that he'd been 'busy.' He's never kept anything from me. Not since Mom's death."

That alone was something. Roy was a straight shooter if ever there was one. The man was too blunt even for the army. It's why he stalled out at Staff Sergeant. He had a bad habit of saying whatever was on his mind, no matter what.

And he didn't spook easily.

"Was he worried about something? Any financial problems?"

"Not that I know of. His pension covered his needs. The house is paid for and he always lived simply."

"New people in his life? Girlfriends? Enemies?"

"You know Dad never dated again, after. And enemies? He was an old man. Who would he have for an enemy?"

"Okay, what about friends?"

"I don't know. Guys at the VFW maybe. Well, and Harry Dunn. I know he and Dad drank together, especially in the winter."

"Who's Harry Dunn?"

"Harold Dunn. I don't really know him. I met him once, twice maybe. And Dad mentioned him a few times, but that's it. He always seemed like kind of a drunk to me, but Dad liked him. Said he made him laugh."

"Any idea where I can find him?"

"I have no idea. Dad didn't keep a Rolodex or anything, and he never got rid of his wall phone. Detested the idea of a cell phone, so it's not like I can look through his call log."

"So no idea?"

"Uhhh, well, I know he was always at the bar he and Dad drank at. I think that's where they met, at Corky's. I picked Dad up there a couple of times. It's on the east side of town."

Taylor nodded, thinking.

“I feel guilty,” Milly said suddenly. “I should have visited more. I only came out on weekends when he wasn’t hunting. Now he’s gone, and I don’t even know what happened to him.”

“You’re here now,” Taylor said. “That counts. Do you want to head back home? Do you have to go back to work?”

“No. I’m not leaving until I can get answers. Until I can bury Dad.”

“Fair enough. Give me your number and the address where you’re staying.”

Milly wrote down her information on a napkin. “What do you think happened to him, Taylor?”

Taylor pocketed the napkin. “Don’t know yet. But I’ll find out.”

“If someone hurt him ...”

“Let’s not get ahead of ourselves. Could be exactly what they’re saying, an accident.”

Taylor didn’t believe that any more than Milly did. The whole thing smelled bad. He could feel it.

“I’ll call you later,” he said, standing up.

Milly nodded. “Be careful. If Dad was into something ... well, just be careful.”

Taylor headed for the door.

The clinic occupied a squat brick building three blocks from the diner, its parking lot empty except for a decade-old Buick and a newer Ford pickup. Taylor pushed through the glass door into a waiting room that smelled of disinfectant and old magazines. The receptionist’s desk sat empty, though there was a bell perched on the counter with a handwritten note that said, “Ring for Service.”

Taylor ignored the bell and walked past the desk into the hallway beyond, checking doors until he found one marked “Dr. D. Henley.”

The door stood slightly open. Taylor knocked twice and entered without waiting for a response.

Doctor Henley sat behind a cluttered desk with a framed photo of a smiling woman and two kids next to his computer monitor, at which he was peering through wire-rimmed glasses. He looked up at the intrusion, his pale blue eyes widening slightly. The man had the soft build of someone who spent too much time sitting and the nervous energy of someone who worried about everything.

"Can I help you?" he asked.

"Doctor Henley? My name is John Taylor. I need to ask some questions regarding Roy Breyer."

Henley fidgeted with a pen, clicking it twice before stopping. "Yes, well, it's a complicated situation. There's a ... a lot of paperwork. Are you with the family's legal counsel?"

"I'm investigating his death," Taylor said, deciding to be as nonspecific as he could and let the doctor fill in his own facts. "The family has questions regarding his death, and were only recently told it was accidental. Is that your official finding as county coroner?"

"The preliminary finding, yes."

"Preliminary? So you're waiting on a full autopsy report?"

Henley's eyes darted away, toward the window that looked out on a brick wall. "That's the thing ... you see, I mean, well, the autopsy hasn't been performed yet."

Taylor let a moment of silence pass. "Mr. Breyer died over the weekend, maybe as early as Friday, and it is now Tuesday. Why hasn't an autopsy been performed on a death you're already calling accidental?"

"The sheriff's department put a hold on it," Henley said the words quickly, as if hoping to push them past Taylor without inspection. "Until Sheriff Brody gives the clearance, my hands are tied."

"That's an unusual procedure. In most jurisdictions, the medical examiner or coroner operates independently of law enforcement. They determine whether an autopsy is required, and when it's performed. It is a medical decision, not a police one. Most jurisdictions actually have requirements, I believe, for how long you're allowed to wait until that determination is made. Especially when there's no active criminal investigation."

Henley's face flushed. The pen in his hand was now being rolled between his thumb and forefinger. "Well, this is Glacier Falls, not Minneapolis. We have our own way of doing things. Sheriff Brody requested we wait."

"Why? Did he give a reason? If he suspects foul play, then you shouldn't be calling it an accident. If he doesn't suspect foul play, then he has no reason to interfere with your duties. Which is it, Doctor?"

The logic was simple, and anyone who got as far as medical school would understand it. Henley certainly did, as his soft exterior seemed to shrink in on itself. He put the pen down and steepled his fingers, a gesture that was meant to look thoughtful but just looked defensive.

"I am not at liberty to discuss the specifics of an ongoing ... inquiry."

"What kind of accident was it?"

"I can't ..."

"Was it a fall?" Taylor asked. "A vehicle collision? An equipment malfunction? Roy was a healthy man. He didn't just drop dead."

"Look, I understand the family is grieving, but there is a protocol for these things."

"The protocol is for you to do your job. You determine the cause of death, you write your report, and you release the body to the next of kin. It's been four days. The family wants to make arrangements. Your delay is causing them considerable distress."

Henley's composure finally fractured. "And who exactly are you? You come in here asking questions, quoting jurisdictions ... are you from the state board? The Attorney General's office?"

Taylor couldn't tell if he was afraid of the answer or wanted it. If he was involved somehow, he wouldn't want anyone from the state being involved. If he was more of a patsy, and everything about him suggested to Taylor that he was definitely that type and not the kind of guy who made any of his own decisions, then an official investigation would take the decision out of his hands.

But, he'd also asked a direct question. Taylor had hoped he'd go on believing that he was there in some official capacity, but to actually say he was with the state or law enforcement would bring a whole new set of problems that could complicate matters.

"I'm a friend of the family," Taylor said plainly.

The effect was instantaneous. The doctor's posture changed as he realized he might not be in any actual trouble after all. The soft, doughy man found a spine, even if it was a weak one.

"A friend?" Henley scoffed. "You have no authority here. You can't just walk in and demand confidential medical information."

It wasn't convincing. The man was sweating, even as he was putting on the affronted face. This was not a man used to confrontation and hoping to bluff his way through.

"I'm not demanding medical information. I'm asking why you aren't doing your job. Mr. Breyer's daughter has a right to know what happened to her father. She has a right to bury him."

"And she will, once everything is cleared with the sheriff," Henley snapped back. He stood up, trying to match Taylor's stance. It didn't work. "I have patient confidentiality to consider. HIPAA regulations. I can't discuss the details of Roy Breyer's death with an unauthorized civilian."

"I'm pretty sure HIPAA is just for a doctor releasing his patient's medical records. A dead man cannot be a patient."

"Regardless, you'll have to talk to the sheriff if you want answers."

"So you'll talk to the sheriff, but not the man's daughter?"

"I have told Ms. Breyer all that I am authorized to tell her at this time. The cause of death has been ruled accidental pending final review."

"And you won't say what kind of accident."

"No," Henley said, his face set in a stubborn mask. "I will not. Not without a court order or direct instruction from Sheriff Brody. Now, if you don't mind, I have a lot of work to do today."

Taylor held the doctor's gaze. He saw only fear there. If he had to guess, it was the fear of a man trapped, a man who had made a bad decision and was now chained to it. Regardless, he wasn't going to get anything else useful here.

"Well then, I guess I'll go see the sheriff," Taylor said.

The sheriff's office shared facilities with the courthouse in the center of town, built in the Classical Revival style every small town in the Midwest liked to use. It apparently made them feel like old America, like DC.

The courthouse was in the center, but a smaller brick building was built to the side of it, extending out to the left of the building, with "Sheriff" in bold letters above the glass doors leading into it. Around the courthouse square were brick shopfronts, the classic

Main Street style, and most of them looked like they'd been empty for a long time.

One had a faded outline where a sign might have said Woolworth's at one time.

Taylor pushed through the glass door and found himself in a cramped reception area with fluorescent lights and the kind of industrial carpeting that had seen better decades.

A deputy sat behind a desk that might have been government surplus from the Carter administration. He was young, maybe twenty-five, with the soft look of someone who'd never been in a real fight. His nameplate read "Deputy Tiller."

"Help you?" Tiller didn't look up from his computer screen.

"I'd like to see the sheriff."

"Sheriff's busy. You got an appointment?"

Taylor waited until the deputy glanced up. "No appointment. Just some questions."

Tiller leaned back in his chair. "Yeah? What about?"

"Roy Breyer's death. I'm trying to get some answers for the family."

The deputy's expression shifted, becoming more guarded. "You some kind of private investigator?"

"Just a friend of the family."

"Uh-huh," Tiller said, looking at him hard for another moment before turning back to his computer, ignoring him. "Sheriff's on a call. Don't know when he'll be free."

Taylor moved closer to the desk. "How about you tell him I'm here? Name's John Taylor."

"Like I said, he's busy."

For as much as he had hated being a cog in the government machine, at this moment, he longed for the badge. It made moments like this significantly less annoying.

The fluorescent light hummed overhead. Somewhere deeper in the building, a phone rang twice and stopped. Taylor let the silence stretch out, watching Tiller pretend to work on whatever was displayed on his monitor.

"Look," Tiller finally said, looking up, particularly annoyed. "I don't know what kind of answers you think you're going to get, but this is an ongoing investigation. We can't just ..."

"What kind of investigation?"

"I can't discuss that," he said, like a kid being caught in a fib.

"Roy Breyer was seventy years old. Lived alone, kept to himself. What exactly are you investigating?"

Tiller glanced toward a hallway that led deeper into the building. "I really can't get into details."

"Then get me someone who can."

"The sheriff's not available."

Taylor remained standing in front of the desk. Tiller went back to his computer, but his movements had become more deliberate, more conscious of being watched.

Another deputy emerged from the hallway, older than Tiller, with gray hair and the kind of belly that spoke of too many years behind a desk. His nameplate identified him as "Deputy Collins."

"Problem here, George?"

"No problem. Just explaining to this gentleman that the sheriff's unavailable. He's asking about Roy Breyer."

Collins looked Taylor up and down. "Roy Breyer?"

"That's right."

"Family hire you?"

"I told your deputy. I'm a friend of the family."

Collins nodded slowly. "Friend of the family. What kind of friend?"

"The kind that doesn't like seeing them get the runaround when their father dies under mysterious circumstances."

"Nothing mysterious about it," Collins said. "Old man had an accident. Happens every day."

"What kind of accident?"

"The accidental kind."

Taylor waited. Collins seemed to enjoy the standoff, the way some men enjoy small exercises of authority.

"I had a visit with Doctor Henley to see about the family getting his body back, and the doctor says he can't release Roy because the sheriff put a hold on it," Taylor said. "The sheriff says it was an accident, which in most places would wrap everything up. Seems like one of those things contradicts the other."

"Does it?"

“Generally speaking, when you know something was an accident, you don’t need to keep investigating it.”

Collins walked around Tiller’s desk, positioning himself between Taylor and the hallway. “Generally speaking, when we’re done with our investigation, we’ll release whatever information we see fit to release.”

“When will that be?”

“When it’s done.”

“His daughter’s trying to plan a funeral.”

“She can plan all she wants. Won’t be having one until we’re satisfied with our findings.”

Taylor felt his jaw tighten but forced himself to stay calm. “Satisfied about what?”

“About whatever we need to be satisfied about.”

Tiller cleared his throat. “Maybe you should come back when the sheriff’s available to meet with you.”

“When would that be?” Taylor asked.

“Hard to say,” Collins replied. “The sheriff’s got a busy schedule.”

Taylor looked at the two of them hard. Tiller looked away, clearly not up for a confrontation, but Collins glared back, almost in challenge.

He was spoiling for some action.

“I’ll come back then I guess.”

Collins and Tiller exchanged a look.

Taylor opened the door. The morning air felt cooler than when he’d arrived, or maybe it was just the contrast with the heated atmosphere inside the sheriff’s office.

“You have a nice day now,” Collins called after him.

Taylor let the door close without responding.

Chapter 3

It took a few minutes of driving around town, which was really all the time it took to cover most of town in total, to find a small L-shaped building with the sign “Pineview Motor Inn” above it. The place looked like it had been built back in the forties and not touched since, but it had a neon sign in the window that said “Vacancy,” which was enough for Taylor. There looked to be about eight units, two on the shorter side of the L with the office anchoring it, and six on the long side, each with a door painted the same faded green.

It had been a long day since he got to the airport in Washington that morning, and the sun was starting to go down as Taylor pulled into the gravel parking lot, stopping in front of the office. Through the window, he could see an elderly woman behind the counter, her gray hair pulled back in a practical bun, reading glasses perched on her nose as she worked on what looked like a crossword puzzle.

A bell chimed when he pushed through the door, causing the woman to look up and set down her pencil.

“Evening. How can I help you?”

“I could use a room for the next few days. Let’s start with three, although I might extend it.”

“Okay,” she said, seeming a little interested in that last part, but also knowing the kind of place this motel was, deciding it was better if she didn’t ask. Instead, she said, “That’ll be two hundred and fifty-nine dollars and twenty cents. Cash or card?”

“Cash.” Taylor pulled two hundreds and a few twenties from his wallet and set them on the counter while he filled out the card.

He used his real name but kept the address section minimal. He hadn't exactly kept a low profile so far, so hiding his identity now didn't seem to make much sense.

"You're not from around here." It wasn't a question. The woman counted out his change and handed him a key attached to a plastic diamond with the number four printed on it.

"Just passing through."

"Room four's right in the middle there. Ice machine's next to the office, if you need it."

Room four smelled of Pine-Sol and stale cigarette smoke. The furnishings were simple. A double bed with a faded floral comforter, a small round table with two chairs, and an old tube television sitting on a dresser. It was clean enough. He dropped his duffel bag on the luggage rack, locked the deadbolt, and drew the heavy polyester curtains shut. The room went dark except for the thin line of light coming through where the curtains met.

He took his laptop from the bag, set it on the small table, and plugged it in. While it booted, he retrieved his sidearm from the locked hard case in his luggage, did a quick check, as was his habit, and set it on the nightstand within easy reach of the bed. He wasn't exactly expecting trouble, but that didn't mean trouble wouldn't come looking for him.

The motel's Wi-Fi was slow, but it worked. Taylor opened a browser and started with the obvious, searching for whatever paper they might have in Glacier Falls, Minnesota. It didn't take long to realize a town with a population that wouldn't fill a city block back east wouldn't have its own newspaper. The next level up was the Flathead County Chronicle, the paper that covered the entire county, including several equally tiny towns. Its website was a cluttered mess of local ads for farm equipment, diners and syndicated pop-up ads that made it hell to navigate.

Here was the first snag. He actually had no idea what he was looking for. All he knew was that it was weird that they weren't releasing the body, and everyone involved was acting sketchy about it.

Not exactly something they had a section for.

That meant hours of just reading through random articles until he started getting a pattern for the place. Taylor started with the past week's news and worked his way back. Most of it was the mundane rhythm of small-town life. A prolonged and bitter dispute over library funding, several stories about the basketball team from one town over that was having a pretty decent season, a pretty bitter dispute over some mining rights on the other side of the county, a Bureau of Land Management inspector who'd apparently been missing for a few weeks, and some articles on seasonal road closures in the area.

Nothing that would connect to Roy, at least not in a way Taylor could see.

He kept digging, pushing further back into the archives. Two months. Four months. Six months. He ignored the birth announcements and wedding notices, the school honor rolls and the classifieds, focusing on police reports, town news, and the one section newspapers never failed to update, the obituaries.

That was where he started to see something interesting. While the county as a whole had a fair number of deaths over the last year or two, they were mostly spread all over.

Not all of them were, however.

About five months ago, Justin Bradley, a rancher on the outskirts of town, had died in a single-car accident late at night when his truck had gone off the road and hit a tree. The death was listed as a suicide, and he was survived by a wife and two children. It was close enough that Dr. Henley would have been the one to do the autopsy.

Then there was Thomas Evans, fifty-seven, who was killed in some kind of hunting accident around the same time. It happened in the hills just outside of town and was also ruled a tragic accident, no charges were filed.

The more he looked, the more the list grew.

Three months ago, there was Sarah Miller, thirty-five, who worked in the local schools and was a hiker. She'd apparently been on a treacherous trail in the same hills where Evans died, where she'd slipped and fallen to her death. Her body was recovered by search teams two days later. Another terrible accident, mourned widely since she was apparently popular with students and colleagues.

After her was Peter Olsen, sixty-two, who ran a small engine repair shop in town and had been found floating in the river after going out fishing, and then three weeks ago, Ryan Hall, fifty-one. There'd been some kind of accidental fire in one of the barns on his farm that he'd tried to put out on his own. By the time the volunteer fire department had responded, the structure was already fully engulfed. They found Jensen's body inside after they put the blaze out.

Again, after an investigation, Dr. Henley and the sheriff had ruled the death a freak accident.

When he added Roy's death to the mix, that was six dead people from accidents in as many months. The national average for accidental deaths was somewhere around sixty per one hundred thousand people per year. For a town of eighteen hundred, the statistical expectation would be about one accidental death per year. Maybe two in a bad year.

Six in six months was not a bad year; it was a big red flag.

Just to make sure, he went back and looked through several more months of obituaries, but found accidents were more in the range of one every six months to a year, just like the national averages suggested. Most deaths out here were caused by two things: natural causes and drug overdoses.

Six in six months was not a bad year. It was a statistical impossibility.

These were not the slow declines of old age or the ravages of long-term illness. These were sudden, violent ends. A car crash. A gunshot wound. A long fall. A drowning. A fire. And now Roy, dead from an accident so secret no one could even name it.

The causes were all different, and there was no obvious connection between the dead that he could see, at least on paper. They had a rancher, a hunter, a teacher, a mechanic, a farmer, and a retired army vet. Their ages, sexes, races, and ethnicities all varied.

The only thing they had in common was that they lived in Glacier Falls, their deaths were investigated by the sheriff's department and ruled accidents, and their post-mortems were done by Dr. Henley.

Whatever was going on, he'd bet a dollar there was something else that connected them all. He could feel it, which meant it was time to do some poking around.

That would have to wait for tomorrow, though. Tonight, he needed to get to this bar Milly mentioned and talk to Roy's friend, see if he knew what Roy had been up to. It bothered Taylor that Roy hadn't told his daughter. The last time they'd talked, the two had been very close, and if something that important was going on, he would have told her about it.

The only reason he could think of that he wouldn't have told her was if he thought it might be dangerous and wanted to keep her safe.

And it looked like he'd been right.

Taylor checked his watch, half past seven. Time to head over to Corky's and see what Roy's friend, Harold, might know. He closed his laptop and grabbed his jacket.

The drive across town took all of five minutes. He realized he'd actually passed Corky's once, just hadn't registered it as a bar. It was only two blocks from the courthouse, which was only two blocks from the edge of the town proper.

There really just wasn't that much town.

Although, it wasn't as completely podunk as it might seem. He noticed two security cameras mounted under the eaves covering the front entrance and parking area.

So it at least had a foot in the twentieth century. Maybe twenty-first if they were Wi-Fi.

Inside, the bar was just a bar. It had that familiar smell of stale beer and cigarettes, which made it stand out from places back east where you couldn't smoke inside. Dark wood paneling covered the walls, and a dozen mismatched tables filled the space between the entrance and a long bar that ran along the back wall. Maybe twenty people scattered throughout, most probably regulars.

Taylor approached the bartender, a heavy-set woman in her fifties with graying hair pulled back in a ponytail.

"What can I get you?"

"Beer. Whatever you have on tap." Taylor settled onto a barstool. "I'm looking for Harry Dunn."

She filled a glass with Budweiser and set it in front of him.

"Harry's over there," she said, nodding toward a corner table where a man in his sixties sat alone, staring into a half-empty whiskey glass.

Taylor paid for his beer and walked over. "Mind if I sit?"

Harry looked up. Weathered face, gray stubble, and the kind of tired eyes that came from too many years of hard work. "Depends who's asking."

"John Taylor. I knew Roy from the army."

"Yeah?" Harry gestured to the empty chair across from him. "Not many of those friends coming around these days."

Taylor sat down and took a sip of his beer. "Yeah, that's how it goes sometimes. Milly called me and told me what happened. I'm sorry about Roy."

"What happened is a load of horseshit. Roy didn't die in no accident."

"What makes you say that?"

"Because he wouldn't. You knew him. Never was a harder man ever made. Guy could live on nails and boot leather. He was smart, careful, and didn't mess around. He'd never just trip and fall or whatever."

Taylor leaned forward. "Do you know what he was doing before his ... accident?"

Harry glanced around the bar, then back at Taylor. "You really knew Roy?"

"Yeah. Met him when I was wet behind the ears. He kicked the shit out of me and taught me to be a man."

"That's Roy for ya," he said, seemingly satisfied. "And no, not really, except that he was doing something and asking questions."

"What do you mean? What kind of questions?"

"He said something wasn't right and he was gonna look into it. He didn't say what it was, but he said he was going to head up into the hills and look into it."

"You guys have a lot of hills around here. Do you know where, exactly, he was looking?"

"He didn't say. I don't know if he wasn't sure and was just poking around, or if he was just protecting all of us by keeping it close. Roy could go either way."

"Yeah, I know how he could be."

"Wish I could be more help, but Roy didn't say anything. All I know is that whatever he was looking into, it's why he's dead. Not some accident."

"It's okay. I have a few other areas I can look into. I'll figure out what he was doing and get his body back to Milly so he can be put to rest. You have my word on it."

Harry looked up at him. "You really think you can find out what happened to him?"

"I'm going to try."

"Then watch your back. Whatever Roy stumbled onto, whatever 'they' are doing, it's worth killing for. If they did Roy, who lived here, they'll do a stranger like you without a second thought."

"They can try," Taylor said, standing up and putting a few bills on the table for the next round. "Won't be the first, probably won't be the last."

Nodding to Harry, Taylor turned and headed out.

The temperature had dropped since Taylor had gone into the building. He zipped up his jacket, thinking everything over.

He still didn't have a handle on what was happening here, only that there was something happening. His conversation with Harry had given him more questions than answers, but at least now he knew Roy had been investigating something in the hills before he died.

It was quiet. Most of the businesses along Main Street had already closed for the night, their windows dark.

Taylor had his keys out and was twenty feet from his car when he heard the low rumble of an engine behind him. He turned around immediately, but his peripheral vision caught the distinctive light bar mounted on top of the approaching vehicle: a sheriff's department cruiser.

The car pulled into the lot and stopped at an angle that blocked Taylor's path to his rental. The engine shut off, and Taylor heard the creak of a door opening. Heavy footsteps approached across the gravel.

"Evening," came a voice from behind him.

Taylor turned. The man walking toward him wore a tan uniform stretched tight across a considerable belly and wore a nameplate that read "Brody." The sheriff moved with the kind of asshole swagger he'd seen from small-town cops before.

A man used to being the big fish in a really small town.

"Sheriff," Taylor said.

Brody stopped about six feet away, close enough to make the encounter feel confrontational without being overtly aggressive. He hooked his thumbs in his duty belt and looked Taylor up and down with small, weaselly eyes.

"My deputies mentioned you paid them a visit this afternoon," Brody said. "They also said that you didn't mention your name."

"They didn't ask. It's Taylor. John Taylor."

"John Taylor." Brody repeated the name like he was testing how it sounded. "Is that name supposed to mean something to me?"

"No reason it should."

Brody nodded slowly, but Taylor could see when something ticked in the man's head. Taylor cursed his sometimes high profile. This guy might be an asshole, almost certainly was, but he wasn't a complete idiot like his two deputies. He'd think he heard Taylor's name before and he'd look him up.

Taylor was almost certain of it.

"They also mentioned you had some questions about Roy Breyer's death."

Taylor met the sheriff's stare without blinking. "I do."

"Interesting." Brody shifted his weight, and his hand moved closer to his service weapon. Not threatening, exactly, but making sure Taylor noticed where it was. "See, Roy Breyer died in an accident. Tragic, but these things happen. No need for anyone to go stirring up trouble for his family."

"His daughter asked me to find out what happened to him."

"Did she now? Well, I can save you some time. Like I said, it was an accident. Case closed."

"Not exactly closed. What kind of accident? Where? And why won't you release his body?" Taylor asked.

"You're not from around here, Mr. Taylor. People in small towns don't much care for strangers showing up and causing problems."

"I'm not causing problems. I'm asking legitimate questions about a man's death."

"Questions that have already been answered."

"Have they? Because until yesterday, his daughter hadn't even been told that it was an accident, and your department still won't release the body to his family for burial. That seems like a lot of unanswered questions."

"There are procedures to follow. Paperwork. These things take time."

"Four days for an accident?"

Brody's smile disappeared completely. "You seem awfully interested in police procedures for a civilian. What exactly is your background, Mr. Taylor?"

"I do security work," Taylor said, unhelpfully.

If he wanted more, he'd need to do his own legwork.

"Security work." Brody made it sound vaguely distasteful. "What kind of security work?"

"The kind that pays the bills."

Brody's eyes narrowed. He was getting frustrated with Taylor's non-answers, which Taylor could relate to. If he didn't want to give answers, then he didn't deserve any.

"You know what I think, Mr. Taylor? I think you're the kind of man who makes a living off other people's grief. Probably promised Roy's daughter all kinds of things to get her to hire you. How much is she paying you? Now there's a case worth looking into."

"She's not paying me anything. I'm an old family friend. I knew Roy back when he was in the army. An old enough friend to know Roy was a good man, and his daughter deserves to know what happened to him."

"His daughter needs to accept that sometimes bad things happen to good people. That's life." Brody's tone suggested the conversation was over. "My advice to you is to wish her well and head back to wherever you came from. Tonight would be good."

"And if I don't?" Taylor asked.

Brody's smile returned. "Well, that would be unfortunate."

"I'm staying at the Pineview Motor Inn," Taylor said. "Room twelve. If you need to find me."

Brody blinked, clearly not expecting Taylor to volunteer his location. But it wasn't like there were a lot of places to stay, and even a small force like the one here would be able to track him to the only motel in town.

"That's ... helpful of you."

"Just being cooperative."

"Right." Brody studied Taylor's face, trying to read him. "You know, Mr. Taylor, I'm starting to get the feeling you're not taking me seriously."

"I'm taking you very seriously, Sheriff."

Brody's face flushed red. "You've got a smart mouth for someone in your position."

"What position is that?"

"Alone. In a town where nobody knows you. A long way from home. Accidents happen all the time around here, Mr. Taylor. Sometimes to locals. Sometimes to visitors who don't know how to mind their own business. You and Ms. Breyer should keep that in mind."

"That sounds like a threat, Sheriff."

"Just a friendly warning from one professional to another." Brody adjusted his belt again. "I'd hate for anything to happen to either one of you while you're visiting our little town."

Taylor looked around the parking lot. A few cars passed on the street, but no one was paying attention to their conversation.

"I appreciate the warning," Taylor said.

"Listen to it. I don't want to see you in this town tomorrow night."

Taylor didn't answer, just continued staring at the man. Brody stared right back for another long moment, clearly frustrated that his intimidation tactics weren't having the desired effect. Finally, he turned and walked back to his cruiser. The engine started with a roar, and he backed out of the parking lot with unnecessary speed, tires spinning on the gravel.

Taylor watched the taillights disappear down Main Street, then looked around the parking lot one more time. The encounter had confirmed some of his suspicions about Sheriff Brody, but it had also raised new questions.

Considering how the investigation had gone so far, Taylor already suspected the police and the doctor were involved in something shady, so that confirmation added little to the picture he was building.

Neither did the threats. Once they started circling the wagons, it was obvious that would be next. If Roy was looking into something and they killed him because of it, they wouldn't stop at just one.

Taylor got into his rental car and pulled out of the parking lot. He had barely turned down the street when he caught a glimpse of the sheriff's cruiser parked at the far end of Main Street. Watching. Waiting. Making sure he knew he was being monitored.

Fine. Let Brody watch. Taylor had operated in hostile territory before, and he'd faced significantly scarier men than the sheriff.

All the fat man had done was motivate him.

Whatever Roy had discovered in those hills, Taylor was going to find it and get justice for his friend. And if Sheriff Brody tried to stop him, well ... that would be unfortunate for Sheriff Brody.

Chapter 4

Taylor arrived at the courthouse just after eight-thirty the next morning. The building's main entrance led to a lobby with marble floors that looked like whoever designed it and used taxpayer money to pay for it had imagined a much grander place than where the building actually sat.

A directory on the wall listed the various county offices, and Taylor found what he needed: County Clerk and Recorder, second floor.

At the top of the stairs, a hallway stretched in both directions, lined with frosted glass doors bearing black lettering. He found the clerk's office halfway down the hall and pushed through the door.

The room was larger than he expected, with rows of filing cabinets along one wall and a counter separating the public area, which had a few computer terminals, from the workspace beyond. A woman in her forties sat behind the counter, typing at a computer. She looked up when Taylor approached.

"Help you?"

"I need to look at property records," Taylor said. "Public records search."

"What property?"

"Several. I'm researching land sales in the area over the past two years."

The woman studied him for a moment, then gestured toward a computer terminal near the window. "You can use that station. The system's pretty straightforward. If you need help, let me know."

Taylor settled into the chair and switched on the terminal. The interface was dated but functional. He started with Roy's property, entering the address Milly had given him. The record pulled up quickly.

Roy had owned forty-three acres along the Missouri River, purchased in 1998 for eighty-five thousand dollars. The land included river frontage and extended back into wooded hills. No sales recorded. No liens. The property remained in Roy's name.

Taylor printed the record and moved on to the next name from his list. Thomas Evans, the hunter who'd died in an accident five months ago. The search took longer this time, but eventually Taylor found it, one hundred and twelve acres in the same general area as Roy's property, also with river access.

Evans had owned the land since 2003. But six weeks after his death, the property had sold to something called Mountain Vista Industries for four hundred thousand dollars.

Taylor added that to his notes and searched for Sarah Miller, the teacher who'd fallen to her death three months ago. She hadn't owned property. Neither had Ryan Hall, the farmer who'd died in the barn fire. But Peter Olsen, the mechanic who'd drowned, had owned sixty-eight acres. It sold two months after his death to Mountain Vista Industries for three hundred and twenty thousand.

Justin Bradley, the rancher whose truck had gone off the road, had owned the largest parcel, two hundred and forty acres stretching along the river and up into the hills. That property sold a month after his death to Mountain Vista Industries for seven hundred and fifty thousand dollars.

Three deaths. Three sales. All to the same buyer.

Taylor sat back and pictured the data as a whole in his head. Roy's property hadn't sold yet, but the others had moved quickly after their owners died. Too quickly, really. Estate sales usually took months to settle, especially when deaths were unexpected. But these properties had changed hands within weeks.

He pulled up the map function and plotted the locations. The properties formed a rough line along the Missouri River, each one adjacent or nearly adjacent to the next. Together, they represented nearly five hundred acres of continuous riverfront land.

Taylor expanded his search, looking for other properties in the same area that hadn't been involved in deaths. He found four more parcels along the same stretch of river. Two had sold to Mountain Vista Industries in the past eighteen months, although neither of those was associated with deaths. The other two remained with their original owners.

The woman at the counter glanced over. "Finding what you need?"

"Yeah. Have you ever heard of Mountain Vista Industries?"

"Of course, they've been one of the largest employers around here for years, although they used to be called Mountain Vista Mining."

"Mining?"

"This whole area used to be mining country. Copper, mostly. Mountain Vista was one of the bigger operations, but the mines played out in the nineties and they were just hanging on, slowly shutting down shafts for the next fifteen years. About, I don't know, three years ago or so, the son took over the operation and they started working on some environmental thing. It must be going good because they've been hiring again, which I'll tell you is a big relief for a lot of people around here."

"What kind of environmental work?"

"Not sure exactly, something about clean energy or some green stuff like that. They built a new facility on the edge of town about two years ago. Big investment."

Taylor made notes. "You said this all started when the son took over?"

"Wade Hutchins. His family's been in the mining business here for generations. His grandfather started the original company back in the fifties, but when Wade took over, he made some changes. Or so I heard."

Taylor thanked her and returned to the computer. He searched for more information about Mountain Vista Industries, but the county records only showed business filings and property transactions. The company had purchased eight properties in the past two years, all along the Missouri River. He already knew several of those had belonged to the people who died, but just as many people sold without anything bad happening to them.

He pulled up the business registration, which confirmed what the clerk had said. Mountain Vista Mining, incorporated in Montana, did a name and purpose change three years ago to Mountain Vista Industries, with its primary business listed as "environmental remediation and waste reclamation services." Corporate officers included Wade Hutchins as CEO and two others Taylor didn't recognize.

The company's registered address matched a location on the outskirts of Glacier Falls. Taylor made note of it.

He went back to the map and studied the properties. It seemed pretty clear that Mountain Vista had been systematically acquiring land along a specific stretch of the river. They'd purchased some properties through normal sales, or at least sales that appeared normal on paper, if paying a bit more than he thought they should go for, but about half had been after the owners died in accidents.

Six deaths in five months. Five properties that either had sold or likely would sell to Mountain Vista. That wasn't a coincidence.

Taylor searched for death certificates, but those records weren't publicly available. He'd need a court order or family permission to access them. What he could access were the property tax records, which showed when payments had been made and by whom.

Thomas Evans's property taxes had been paid by Mountain Vista Industries within days of the sale closing. Same with Peter Olsen's land and Justin Bradley's ranch. The new owner had moved fast to secure the properties and keep them current.

Taylor leaned back and rubbed his eyes. He'd been staring at the screen for over two hours, but the picture was getting clearer. Mountain Vista wanted this land badly enough to pay premium prices for it. They wanted it badly enough that they'd acquired most of it right after the owners died in suspicious accidents.

The question was why. What made this particular stretch of river so valuable?

He pulled up maps of the area. The properties ran along the Missouri River for roughly eight miles, starting just west of Glacier Falls and extending into the hills. Dense forest covered most of the land, with the river cutting through the valley bottom. He could see old mining roads and what might be closed shaft entrances on some of the properties, remnants of the area's mining history.

Taylor zoomed in on the Mountain Vista facility, which on this map was still only partially built. God, he missed having things like satellite imagery.

The new building sat on the southern edge of the company's land holdings, right where the river came down from the hills. The structure looked like it was going to be large, or was large now that it was built, with what looked like several smaller outbuildings and a paved parking area. A service road connected it to the main highway.

The company had systematically acquired land along a specific corridor. They'd built a major facility at the downstream end of that corridor. And they'd done it all within the past two years, most of it in the past eighteen months.

The same eighteen months when six people had died in accidents.

It at least gave him somewhere to start. Roy had been onto something, and if Taylor had to guess, it was looking into the deaths of his neighbors. If Roy had been killed for that or for his land, which was in the stretch Mountain Vista was buying up, Taylor didn't know yet.

What he did know was they were somehow involved. There were too many coincidences for it not to be.

Taylor gathered his papers and stood up. The woman at the counter looked over.

"Done already?"

"For now. Thanks for your help."

"Find what you were looking for?"

"More than I expected," Taylor said.

He walked out of the clerk's office and down the stairs.

Taylor needed to see these properties for himself.

He found the Bradley ranch ten miles north of Glacier Falls, where the county road turned to gravel. The house sat back from the road, a single-story ranch with faded blue siding and a detached garage. A Ford pickup with rust eating through the wheel wells sat in the driveway next to a U-Haul trailer, already half-loaded with boxes and furniture.

He parked behind the pickup and got out. The property stretched down toward the river that ran perpendicular to the property, east to west. It was maybe forty acres of cleared land with pine forest hemming it in on three sides. Fresh wooden stakes dotted the landscape, bright orange flags tied to each one. Survey markers. Recent ones, from the look of them.

The front door opened before Taylor reached the porch. A woman in her fifties stood in the doorway, gray-streaked brown hair pulled back in a ponytail. She wore jeans and a flannel shirt with rolled-up sleeves, work gloves on her hands. Her eyes went from Taylor to his car and back again.

"Can I help you?"

"Mrs. Bradley?"

"Who's asking?"

Taylor stopped at the bottom of the porch steps. "My name's John Taylor. I'm looking into some property transactions in the area."

"Property's already sold," she said, moving to close the door.

"I'm not here to buy. Just want to ask a few questions about your sale."

Her hand froze on the door. "What kind of questions?"

"The kind that might help me understand what happened to Roy Breyer."

She blinked. "Roy's dead."

"I know. I'm looking into his death for his daughter."

Mrs. Bradley looked past Taylor toward the road, then back at him. Her fingers drummed against the door's frame. "You're not from around here."

"No."

"Then maybe you should head back to wherever you came from."

Taylor didn't move. "Roy was a friend. I owe it to him to find out what happened."

"Roy had an accident. That's what everyone says."

"You believe that?"

She didn't answer right away. Her eyes flicked toward the tree line, then back to Taylor. "Doesn't matter what I believe. He's dead either way."

"How well did you know him?"

"Well enough to know he didn't deserve what happened." She caught herself, pressed her lips together. "Look, I've got packing to do. I need to be out of here by the end of the week."

"Where are you moving?"

"Sioux Falls."

Taylor glanced at the U-Haul. "That's a long way from home."

"Sometimes that's what you need."

"You selling because you want to or because you have to?"

"I don't see how that's any of your business."

"Mountain Vista Industries bought this place."

It wasn't a question, but her reaction was clear as day. Her shoulders drew up, and she took a half step back into the house. "I really need to get back to packing."

"Your husband died five months ago in a car accident on Highway 89."

"Yes."

"Sheriff Brody investigated."

"That's his job."

"Doctor Henley ruled it accidental."

She said nothing.

Taylor moved up one step. "I've been looking at property records. Mountain Vista's been buying up land along the river. A lot of it from families who lost someone in an accident. Your husband. Tom Evans."

"I don't know anything about that."

"You know Mountain Vista bought this property."

"Lots of companies buy property. That's how it works."

"How much did they pay you?"

"That's private."

"Was it a fair price?"

"It was enough."

"Enough for what?"

"Enough to get out of here and start over somewhere I don't have to ..." She stopped, shook her head. "Look, I really have a lot to do."

Taylor waited, let the silence stretch. Whatever she was afraid of, it wasn't standing in her driveway.

"Did someone threaten you?"

"No one threatened anyone. I just ... I decided it was time to sell. That's all."

"Right after your husband died."

"I can't run this place alone. The ranch was his dream, not mine."

"So Mountain Vista made you an offer."

"They made an offer. I accepted. End of story. They've bought up a lot of property around here. Property from people who are alive and well, too, before you go getting conspiratorial."

Taylor glanced at the survey stakes again. "They've already been out here marking things up."

"They can do what they want. It's their property now."

"What are they doing with it?"

"I don't know."

"You didn't ask?"

"Why would I? I'm leaving."

"Because maybe you're curious why someone would pay cash for a working ranch and then let it sit empty."

Mrs. Bradley's hand moved to the door again. "I need to go."

"One more question."

"I've answered enough."

"Did Roy ever come out here? Talk to you about anything?"

"No."

"You sure about that?"

"I said no. Now get off my property."

Taylor nodded, descended the steps. He walked back toward his car, then paused and turned. Mrs. Bradley still stood in the doorway, watching him. "If you remember anything that might help ..."

"I won't."

"Where can I reach you in Sioux Falls?"

"You can't."

She went inside and shut the door. The deadbolt snicked home a moment later.

Taylor sat in his car and studied the property. The survey stakes formed a rough perimeter around the cleared land, extending down toward the river. A small metal sign near the driveway read: PROPERTY OF MOUNTAIN VISTA INDUSTRIES - NO

TRESPASSING. The sign looked new, the metal still bright and unfaded.

He pulled out his phone and took several photos of the stakes, the sign, and the general layout. Mrs. Bradley was scared, and not just of him. Someone had gotten to her, made it clear what would happen if she talked.

The question was, what had Roy found that made him worth killing?

Taylor started the car and headed back to the county road. The Hendricks property was another eight miles north, closer to the river. According to the property records, it had sold to Mountain Vista three months after Ryan Hall's death in a barn fire.

The Hendricks place was easier to find. A large hand-painted sign at the entrance read: MOUNTAIN VISTA INDUSTRIES PRIVATE PROPERTY - AUTHORIZED PERSONNEL ONLY. The gate stood open, though, and no one seemed to be around to enforce the warning.

Taylor drove in. The main house was bigger than the Bradley place, a two-story farmhouse with a wraparound porch and a red metal roof. Empty. The windows dark, no vehicles in sight. A barn and several outbuildings stood behind the house, their doors hanging open or missing entirely.

He parked in front of the house and got out. The place had the abandoned feel of somewhere people left in a hurry and never came back to. Weeds pushed up through cracks in the concrete walkway. Someone's home, once. Now it was just another piece of property on Mountain Vista's growing list.

Taylor walked the perimeter of the house, looking in windows. Furniture remained in some rooms, covered with dust. Whatever had happened here, the Hendricks family hadn't taken much with them when they left.

There were survey stakes here too, dozens of them forming a grid pattern across the property. They ran down the sloping lawn toward the river, which Taylor could see through the trees. More stakes marked the tree line itself, suggesting Mountain Vista's plans extended into the forest.

He walked down toward the water. The ground dropped away sharply about fifty yards from the house, a steep embankment that led to the river's edge. Someone had built stairs down to the river at one point, but they'd rotted through in places. Taylor descended carefully, testing each step before putting his weight on it.

The river moved slow and brown, about thirty yards across at this point. On the far bank more trees loomed. Upstream, he could make out the roof of another building through the foliage, maybe a mile away. Downstream, the water curved out of sight around a bend.

Taylor studied the bank. Fresh tire tracks in the mud, recent enough that rain hadn't washed them away yet. Wide tracks, like a truck or heavy equipment. They came down from a path through the trees to his right, stopped at the water's edge, then looped back up the same way.

He followed the tracks. The path wound through the forest, clearly used enough to stay clear of undergrowth. After about a hundred yards, it opened into a small clearing where the tire marks became more numerous, overlapping and cutting deep into the soft earth. Someone had been using this spot regularly for something that required heavy vehicles.

But for what? Taylor saw no signs of construction, no equipment, no materials. Just the tracks and the trampled ground.

He returned to the riverbank and looked upstream again. The building he'd spotted earlier might be worth investigating, but that would require crossing private property, possibly multiple parcels.

Taylor climbed back up the embankment and walked to the barn. The double doors stood open wide enough for him to enter without touching them. Inside, the space was empty except for old hay bales stacked against one wall and farm equipment that looked like it hadn't been run in years.

He checked the other outbuildings. A machine shed with nothing in it. A chicken coop that hadn't housed chickens in months, judging by the dried droppings. A small workshop with tools still hanging on pegboards, a calendar on the wall showing May of the previous year.

The whole place felt wrong. Not just abandoned ... evacuated. Like the Hendricks family had been told to leave, leave now, and take only what they could carry. Mountain Vista had bought the property, bought it fast, and the family had disappeared. No forwarding address in the county records. No indication where they'd gone.

Taylor walked back to his car. He pulled out his phone and took photos of everything: the house, the barn, the survey stakes, the tracks leading down to the river. Then he sat behind the wheel, thinking.

Mountain Vista was buying riverfront property as fast as they could acquire it. They were paying cash, moving quickly, and the families selling the properties either ended up dead or running scared to other states. The company was surveying everything, marking boundaries, asserting control. But they weren't developing the land, weren't building anything visible. Just, claiming it.

Roy must have figured out what they were doing. He'd gone up into the hills, Harry had said. Found something worth killing for. Whatever it was, it connected to the river, these properties, and the systematic elimination of anyone who got too close to the truth.

Taylor started the car and headed back toward town. There was something he'd noticed when he'd been looking over the deed sales. A fairly large property east of town, closer to the hills, that had not sold.

One of the few, and Taylor wanted to know why.

Chapter 5

While there were still ten properties along this stretch of river that had been sold to Mountain Vista, Taylor had a feeling he was going to get roughly the same information from them as he had from the two he had just seen.

No trespass signs, survey markers, and people leaving in a hurry. What he wanted to see now were the outliers: properties in that stretch that had not been sold.

There were only three in total, and he wanted to see what kind of approaches had been made to them, or if anything else had happened.

The three properties that had not sold yet included Roy's, a property owned by Noah and Carmen Fuller, and one owned by a guy named Pete Kowalski. All three had owned their properties for some time.

There was no reason to visit Roy's. He'd already looked the house over when he first got here, and there was nothing there of note, and Milly would tell him if she was approached to sell.

The Fullers' was the next closest. He pulled out of the Hendricks property and turned west, following the river and moving away from the hills and toward more open country.

The property sat back from the road off a gravel drive that needed grading. Taylor turned in and rolled up to a house that looked lived-in but empty. No truck in the yard. No lights on inside. He killed the engine and sat for a minute, watching the windows.

Nothing moved.

He got out and walked to the front door. Knocked. Waited. Knocked again.

Still nothing.

Taylor walked around the side of the house. The barn doors hung open. Inside, he found stalls but no animals. The feed bins were empty. Dust covered everything. He walked back to the house and looked in a window.

He checked the mailbox at the road. Stuffed full. He pulled out a handful. The postmarks went back two weeks.

It was possible that their property had sold and they had not had a chance to update the records, although there were no survey marks or no trespassing signs.

It was possible that something else had happened, but this was something he would have to look into. Either way, the Fullers had clearly left, which was notable, but did not give him the extra information he actually needed.

He turned and drove back east, toward the hills but still following the river.

As soon as he got to Kowalski's property, he knew this one would be different. The fences were in good repair, and this was the first place he'd seen livestock, with a few cattle visible in the pasture, and there was smoke snaking up from the chimney.

Someone lived here.

He made it thirty yards up the driveway before the first shot kicked up dirt ten feet in front of his rental car.

Taylor hit the brakes and threw the transmission into park. He stayed in the seat, hands visible on the steering wheel. It had been a warning shot to get him to stop. The car was big enough that if they were a threat, the bullet would have at least hit the vehicle.

The shot had come from the direction of the house.

"I am not here to cause trouble," Taylor called out the open window.

Another shot. This one closer. Maybe five feet from the front bumper.

"Turn around and get the hell off my property," a voice yelled from the house.

"I'm looking for Pete Kowalski," Taylor yelled back.

"You found him, now get."

"I'm a friend of Roy Breyer."

Silence. Taylor waited. The car engine ticked as it cooled.

"Roy's dead," the voice said.

"I know, that's why I'm here."

More silence. Then, "You're not from Mountain Vista?"

"No."

"That is what they all say. The last one said it, too. Sure, he wore a fancy suit and had a briefcase, trying to look like a real estate agent, but he didn't fool me. I saw the earpiece and the bulge under his jacket. I know a government operative when I see one."

That was confusing. Nothing Taylor had found suggested Mountain Vista had anything to do with the government.

Taylor kept his hands on the wheel. "I am not with the government."

"A contractor then. That is even worse."

"I'm not that either. I'm a friend of Roy's; I served with him in the army."

"Prove it."

Taylor thought about that. "I am not sure how I can prove I knew Roy twenty years ago."

"Well, then you should just turn around and go."

"Not until I ask you some questions about what is going on around here. I need to find out what happened to Roy and the other people who were killed. Shoot me or talk to me."

That was a risk. The guy sounded kind of unhinged, and he just might shoot him, but he had fired warning shots and talked to him this long, so Taylor was banking on him not actually wanting to shoot anyone.

Taylor had picked out where the guy was, up in a second-floor window. It was a good spot. He had good position, height, and a clear field of fire.

"What is your name?" the voice called.

"John Taylor."

"Are you armed?"

"Yes."

"Of course, you are. They are all armed. Step out of the car. Hands up. And I mean up, not that half-assed shoulder-height nonsense."

Taylor opened the door and got out. He raised his hands over his head.

"Turn around. Full circle. Slow."

Taylor turned.

"Stop. Now walk to the porch. If you reach for anything, I will put one through your chest."

Taylor walked forward. The front door opened, and an old man came out holding a bolt-action rifle. He was seventy if he was a day, with wild gray hair that went in about ten different directions. But the rifle was as steady as Taylor had ever seen.

"Stop there."

Taylor stopped at the bottom of the steps.

Pete Kowalski came down slowly, rifle trained on Taylor's center mass. "Lift your jacket. Both sides."

Taylor did. The Glock sat in its holster at his hip.

"What do you want, G-Man?"

"I'm not with the government."

"That's what they all say." Pete gestured with the rifle. "Inside. Move."

Taylor climbed the steps. Pete stayed back, keeping distance between them so that he could not grab the barrel of his rifle.

They went through the door into a living room that looked like a command center. Papers covered every surface, with maps and newspaper clippings tacked to the wall. There were even a few red strings connecting things.

This guy could be the poster child for whack jobs.

"Sit." Pete pointed to a kitchen chair in the middle of the room.

Taylor sat. Pete moved to a position near the window where he could watch both Taylor and the driveway. The rifle never stopped pointing at Taylor's chest.

"You said you knew Roy."

"That's right."

"When?"

"Eighteen years ago. Before he retired."

"Before he got out of the military-industrial complex."

"Before he left the Army."

Pete's eyes narrowed. "Roy didn't trust easily. He knew what was out there, knew what they were capable of. If he didn't mention you to me, maybe there's a reason."

"Maybe he didn't mention everyone he served with."

"Or maybe you are lying. Do you know what they do? They study you, learn your connections, your history. Then they send someone who fits the pattern so you will believe them and let them past your defenses."

"That seems complicated."

"That's how they operate. They're always tricky, using layers on layers full of misdirection and plausible deniability. They think that I don't know what's going on, but I do. It all fits, with the patents and shell companies, hiding that they're really owned by the government. A place for their black budget projects, out here in the middle of nowhere so no one notices."

Taylor looked at the wall. Photos of helicopters, blurry pics taken of what was probably the completed Mountain Vista facility, and newspaper clippings about the suspicious deaths.

"Tell me about Mountain Vista," Taylor said.

"Which part? The environmental remediation scam? The land grab? The human experimentation? The extraterrestrial technology they are reverse-engineering up in those hills?"

"Start with the land."

Pete laughed. "They want it all. Every acre along this stretch of river. They came to me six months ago and made it look like a legitimate offer, trying to give me market value plus ten percent, but I told them no. No way I was going to sell this place to their type. This land has been in my family for three generations, and it's going to stay that way."

"Did they come back?"

"Yes, four more times. Different people each time, and the offers kept going up. The last one was for market plus thirty percent, in cash, as long as I could close in two weeks, but I know what they were really doing. They were testing me to see if I could be bought. They were trying to find my price. Like hell."

"What happened after you refused?"

"The attacks started." Pete moved to the wall and tapped a calendar covered in red X marks. "At first, it was just some dead fish in the pond. But a few weeks after that, they started going for my cattle."

"Your cattle got sick."

"They did. My dairy cows stopped producing milk. They wouldn't eat right and started losing weight. Then they started stumbling like they were drunk, couldn't stand on their own. You know what that is, right? Neurological damage. They were putting some kind of chemical weapons in my water, trying to see what worked. Probably put it in my water too, but they didn't know I keep a separate stockpile of water. Switched to it when I realized what they were doing so they wouldn't get me too."

"You had them tested?"

"County vet couldn't find anything, but he wouldn't. Not with this government stuff. I sent a sample off to a lab to get tested, but I haven't gotten the sample back yet. I'm betting they don't find anything either. Commercial labs can't check for the kind of military-grade compounds they use. It's all designed to go undetected."

"When did the cows start getting sick?" Taylor asked.

"Four months ago. Right after I turned down their second offer. That's not a coincidence, you know, it's cause and effect. They made an offer, I refused it, and they applied pressure, trying to find my weak point."

"Did anyone else report sick animals?"

"Maybe, but no one's going to tell me. People are afraid and they know what happens when you ask too many questions. It's why most of the people around here don't talk to me unless they have to. Well, except for Roy."

"What do you think happened to Roy?"

"They killed him," Pete said, as if it was the most obvious thing in the world. "I think he got too close and found something they didn't want him to find, so they eliminated him. Probably made it look like an accident, although no one's saying yet. That's how they do it; make it seem like an accident. Car accidents, hunting accidents, heart attacks. They have a whole playbook."

"You sound like you've studied it."

"I've studied everything. That's how you survive. You learn their methods, document their movements, and prepare for when they come for you."

Taylor looked at the maps on the wall. Some had red circles marked around the Mountain Vista facility. Others showed the river and surrounding properties. One had what looked like flight paths drawn in red pen, crisscrossing the entire area in an impossible tangle.

"You mentioned black helicopters," Taylor said.

"Yep, saw them three times in the last month flying over my property at night. No lights, no markings. Stealth jobs that make no noise as they flew, but I knew they were there."

Taylor had been on hundreds of military helicopters, and the one thing they all were was loud. He'd seen stealth fighters, too, and they were only stealth to radar. If one flew near you, you'd know it.

Pete might be right about the accidents, and his livestock might be getting sick, but Taylor had spent a long time working for the government. Enough to know they were terrible at keeping secrets, and if they wanted his property, they would have just come in with eminent domain.

"What about the men you mentioned? The ones sneaking around?"

"I've seen them twice. One time, I caught them creeping around at three in the morning just on the edge of the tree line. Took a shot at them and they ran off into the trees. The other time they were out on the other side of the river, watching me."

Taylor suspected that the people on the other side of the river were supposed to be there, and that Pete shot at shadows in the forest.

"You said Roy came around a few weeks ago."

Pete nodded. "Yeah. He came around about once a month to check on me, make sure I was doing alright and had everything I needed. This last time, though, he was asking questions about my water and if people had been around asking about buying my property."

"What did you tell him?"

"Same thing I'm telling you, that the government's running an operation up in the hills, that they'd tried to buy my property using their front company, and that they were poisoning my water to drive me off my land. I also mentioned I'd seen some of their vehicles up in the hills. Not logging trucks but cargo trucks. The kind that has no business on those switchbacks up there." Pete leaned forward. "Roy wasn't stupid. He noticed the pattern too and knew something was wrong. All those dead people, supposedly from accidents, in less than two years. And all of their property bought up by the same company. No way. Roy saw it, same as us."

So it was us now. The guy wasn't wrong. Crazy, but not wrong. At least about the deaths and land sales.

"You saw trucks up in the hills?"

"I did. I went up there to visit our friend Jake. He used to work for Mountain Vista when they were still a mining company, before the company shit-canned him and closed the mines. I like to take walks up to his place. For my health. I was just coming over a ridge when I saw them. Oh, they were disguised well enough to look like regular work trucks, but I wasn't fooled. You don't bring that kind of truck up into hills like this. Likely as not, they'll get bogged down on one of the dirt roads that're no longer maintained."

"And you told Roy about that?"

"I did."

"Did he say what he was going to do?"

"Yeah. He said he was going to go check it out, visit Jake. That's Jake Morrison."

"Does Jake still live in the hills?"

"He does, down Campbell Road about three miles past the old entrance to shaft number four."

Taylor stood. "Okay. Well, I appreciate the information."

Pete stood too, and he'd stopped pointing the rifle. "You're really going up there?"

"I am."

"You gotta be careful or they'll kill you too, same as they did Roy. Same as they'd do to me if they could get to me."

"I will be."

Taylor walked to the door, with Pete following him out onto the porch.

"Good luck. Hope you catch the bastards."

Taylor waved and walked to his car, Pete's eyes on him the whole time. Pete might be crazy ... no, Pete was definitely crazy, but just because he was nuts didn't mean he wasn't right about some stuff. Almost certainly not about the government connection or black helicopters or people stalking his land late at night, but he was right about the coincidence between all the accidents and the properties bought up by Mountain Vista Industries. He was probably also right about something happening to his animals. Those were his livelihood, and he'd had the vet check them out, but Taylor couldn't figure out yet if their being sick was actually connected or not.

And Roy trusted him, at least enough to check on him and come ask him about what was going on, and that said something. Roy had always been a good judge of people.

Taylor started the car and backed down the drive. In his mirror, he saw that Pete was still standing there, watching and waiting for his black helicopters.

Still, Pete had given him something. Roy had gone up to talk to Jake Morrison, which meant that was Taylor's next stop.

Taylor pulled over onto the shoulder and checked his phone's GPS. Campbell Road didn't exist according to the satellite map, just a tangle of unnamed dirt tracks cutting through the hills. He zoomed in and out, trying different search terms, but got nothing useful. Details for remote areas like this rarely made it into commercial databases. The maps showed topography and a few landmarks, but most of the back roads disappeared into the white space.

He put the rental in drive and turned back toward Glacier Falls. The dashboard clock read eleven-thirty. Time enough to get some lunch and figure out where the hell Campbell Road actually was before he drove up into those hills blind.

Ten minutes later, Taylor pulled his phone out again as he hit the town limits. He scrolled through his contacts and dialed Whitaker.

She picked up on the second ring. "Hey. Everything okay?"

"Yeah. Quick question. Do you have numbers for anyone at the Department of Interior or EPA?"

"Maybe. Why?"

"There's something off with the water and property rights out here. I want to look into it more."

Whitaker was quiet for a moment. "How off?"

"There's a company up here buying up every piece of riverfront property they can get their hands on, including from six people who died in accidents right before their land was sold. If they end up buying Roy's, it will be seven. Roy was apparently asking around about it just before he died, so I want to run it down."

"All right. I'll send you some contact info. Be careful, Taylor."

"Always am."

He ended the call and drove to M&J's Diner, parking in the same spot he'd used the previous morning. The lunch crowd had started to filter in, filling most of the booths, so Taylor took a seat at the counter instead.

The same waitress from the day before appeared with a menu and a glass of water, setting both down in front of him.

"What can I get you?"

"Burger. Medium. Coffee."

She wrote it down and headed for the kitchen. Taylor pulled out the folded county map he'd picked up at the courthouse and spread it across the counter. The hills northwest of town sprawled across the paper in contour lines and elevation markers. Glacier Falls sat in a valley where Blackmouth Creek met the Missouri River. North and west, the terrain rose into forest and ridgelines. A few roads were marked, but Campbell wasn't one of them.

Diane returned with his coffee. Taylor turned the map toward her.

"Do you have any idea where Campbell Road is? I know it's up in these hills northeast of here, but I can't find it."

She leaned over the counter, studying the map. Her finger traced along the main highway out of town, then stopped.

"Don't think I know it. Ray might, though." She called over her shoulder toward the kitchen. "Ray, do you know where Campbell Road is?"

A man emerged from the kitchen, wiping his hands on his apron. Late fifties, thick build, thinning hair; he came around the counter and looked at the map.

"Yeah. I think it has some official number or something, but everyone calls it Campbell now because of the old Campbell place up that way." He tapped a spot on the map about eight miles northwest of town. "Here. Turns off the main highway at mile marker forty-two. Dirt road, heads up into the timber. Follows Blackmouth Creek for a couple miles, then splits. Left fork goes to the Campbell homestead. Right fork keeps going up into the high country."

"Does the right fork go anywhere specific?"

Ray shrugged. "Some cabins and some of the old mine shafts, but they're all shut down now."

"Appreciate it."

Ray nodded and went back to the kitchen. Diane brought Taylor's burger a few minutes later. He ate in silence, thinking through his next moves. Visit Morrison this afternoon, see what Roy had been working on. Check in with Whitaker's contacts at Interior or EPA as soon as she got him the number and dig into Mountain Vista's permits and licenses, although it was doubtful he'd have a signal in the hills, so if she took awhile, he'd have to do it after. Then circle back to what he could prove.

Taylor was halfway through his burger when the man from the booth near the window stood and walked to the register. He paid his bill, exchanged a few words with Diane, then turned toward the door. He stopped when he saw Taylor at the counter and changed direction, walking directly to Taylor.

"Excuse me. You're John Taylor, aren't you?"

Taylor turned on his stool. "That's right."

The man extended his hand. "Wade Hutchins. I thought I recognized you from the news coverage a few years back. The thing with that terrorist in D.C. and then stopping that assassination attempt on the president before she was elected. Pretty impressive stuff."

Sometimes Taylor forgot that he'd been in enough newspapers that people might recognize him. And he was annoyed by it every time he did remember.

Taylor shook his hand. Firm grip, nothing aggressive. So this was Hutchins, the guy listed on the corporate documents he'd read at the courthouse as being the CEO of Mountain Vista Industries.

"Ancient history."

"Still, it's not every day we get someone with your background in Glacier Falls." Hutchins gestured to the empty stool beside Taylor. "Mind if I sit for a minute?"

"Go ahead."

Hutchins settled onto the stool. "So what brings you to our little corner of the world? I'm guessing it's not the tourist season."

"Visiting a friend."

"Anyone I'd know?"

"Doubt it. Old military buddy. Lives out in the hills."

"Ah. We've got a few folks up that way who like their privacy. Can't say I blame them. It's beautiful country."

Taylor sipped his coffee and pointed at Hutchins' shirt that had a Mountain Vista logo on it. "Noticed a lot of signs around here with that logo. Do you work for them?"

"You can say that. I'm the CEO. You must have been out by the river."

"I was. Saw a bunch of your signs on property out there, in fact. Seems like you're buying up a lot of land."

"We've been acquiring some parcels. Part of our expansion plans."

"What kind of business are you in?"

"Industrial services. We've developed some technology that requires significant infrastructure, which is why we need the property."

"Must be expensive."

"It's an investment. We need water access for our operations, and that means securing property rights along the river. You seem pretty well-informed about the local real estate market for someone just visiting a friend."

"I just pay attention, that's all, and it made me curious."

"Curious about what exactly?"

"Why a company needs that much land. Seems like a lot."

Hutchins studied him for a moment. "Depends on the scale of operations. We're positioning ourselves for regional contracts. If we're successful, we'll need the capacity to support that growth."

"I'm surprised you found so many people willing to sell. In my experience, people out in areas like this, working the land, it takes a lot more than money to get them out."

"I guess it depends on how much money they're offered. We pay fair market value plus a premium. I guess everyone has their price." He paused. "You ask a lot of questions for someone who's just curious."

"Old habit."

"You were in law enforcement back then, right? Are you investigating something?"

"Nope. Not with any agency anymore. I do private security now, but I'm just on vacation at the moment."

"Private security, that's interesting. You know, if you're that interested in what we're doing, you should come see the facility. I'm proud of what we've built. It might answer some of those questions you have. And as a business owner, I'd love to hear your thoughts on our security."

Taylor set down his coffee cup. An invitation like this felt like a dodge, maybe trying to throw him off the scent, make it seem like he's being transparent. Whatever it was, it didn't feel on the up and up, but it was an opportunity to see what Mountain Vista was actually doing.

"Are you giving tours now?"

"For someone with your background? Sure," he said, pulling out his wallet and dropping a twenty on the counter. "Does tomorrow morning work for you? Say ten o'clock?"

"I can do that."

"Good. I'll let security know you're coming. Just give them your name at the gate." He stood, his easy smile back in place. "Lunch is on me. Welcome to Glacier Falls, Mr. Taylor."

"That's not necessary."

"I insist." Hutchins held his gaze for another moment. "And I appreciate your service. What you did in D.C. ... that took real courage. We need more people like you willing to step up."

He didn't wait for a response. Hutchins walked to the door, stopped to wave at someone in a corner booth, then headed out into the parking lot. Through the window, Taylor watched him climb into a late-model truck and drive off.

Diane appeared at Taylor's elbow. "More coffee?"

"No thanks."

She picked up Hutchins' twenty and Taylor's empty plate. "That was nice of him."

"Seems like a friendly guy."

"Wade's always been good to folks around here. Even before his company got big." She headed back to the kitchen.

Taylor sat at the counter, thinking. Hutchins had been smooth. Too smooth, maybe. The explanation about infrastructure and water access sounded reasonable enough on the surface, but it didn't explain why he needed such a large footprint. A single facility, no matter how big, shouldn't require a dozen different parcels spread along several miles of riverfront.

Especially since their operations were a couple of miles downriver from those parcels and had already been built.

The invitation bothered him. Hutchins had recognized Taylor from news coverage, knew his background. That meant Hutchins understood Taylor wasn't just some random visitor asking idle questions. Yet he'd offered a facility tour anyway.

Also, the fact was that the doctor and the sheriff were hiding evidence of Roy's death, and the doctor had signed off on all of those other accidents.

Mountain Vista was a big shot in town, with half the county having their paycheck come from them in one way or another, that would swing a lot of weight in a sheriff's election.

A lot of questions and still hardly any answers.

Tomorrow's tour would tell him something, even if it was just how good Hutchins was at hiding whatever Mountain Vista was really doing. But first, he needed to talk to Jake Morrison. Find out what Roy discovered up in those hills. Get the full picture before he walked into Hutchins' facility and gave the man a chance to measure him up close.

He left cash on the counter for the burger and coffee, ignoring Hutchins' twenty, and walked out into the afternoon sun.

Chapter 6

His rental car sat three vehicles down, parked nose-out for a quick exit, one of the habits he'd picked up working with Whitaker. He'd covered maybe ten feet when three men materialized from between a pickup truck and a sedan, spreading across the narrow sidewalk in a loose formation that blocked the path to his car.

Taylor stopped.

The one in the middle stood a few inches over six feet, probably two hundred twenty, with the kind of shoulders that came from actual labor rather than a gym membership. Flannel shirt rolled to the elbows and work boots caked with dried mud. He was somewhere in his forties and his face had the weathered look of someone who spent most of his time outdoors, with deep lines around his eyes and mouth.

The two on either side were younger, probably somewhere in their mid-thirties, and both built lean and hard. The one on the left wore a Carhartt jacket and had his hands stuffed in his pockets. The one on the right kept his arms loose at his sides, weight balanced on the balls of his feet. That one had done this before.

Taylor shifted his stance, angling his body to keep all three in his sight. His right hand hung near his hip, close to the Sig Sauer holstered under his jacket, but he didn't go for it. Not yet.

"Help you?" Taylor asked, keeping his tone conversational.

The big one in the middle spoke. "You're the one asking questions about property around here?"

"That's right."

"Time for you to stop asking."

"Is it?"

"You need to stop bothering people. You're not from around here, and we don't take kindly to strangers. I think it's best if you just go back to wherever you came from and leave all this behind."

Taylor let a few seconds pass, studying their faces. None of them looked away. "Who sent you?"

"Nobody sent us." The one on the right smiled, but there was nothing friendly in it. "Just concerned citizens. We don't like strangers stirring up trouble."

"Strangers like me?"

"Exactly like you." The big one took a half-step forward. "You've been bothering people. That stops now."

Taylor didn't move. "Or what?"

"Or you might have an accident, too."

The one in the Carhartt jacket finally pulled his hands from his pockets, letting them hang at his sides.

"Roads are still icy this time of year. Easy to lose control, especially if you don't know the area."

"Is that supposed to be a threat?"

"Call it friendly advice," the big one said. "Get in your car, drive to Billings, catch a flight home. Forget about Glacier Falls."

Taylor looked past them at his rental car, then back at their faces. "Not going to happen."

The one on the right shifted his weight, hands coming up slightly. "Then we've got a problem."

"Yeah." Taylor's voice stayed level. "We do."

The big one moved first, launching forward with surprising speed for his size. Taylor pivoted left, letting the man's momentum carry him past, and drove his elbow into the exposed ribs. The impact made a solid thump. The big man grunted but kept his feet, spinning back with more control than Taylor had expected.

The one on the right came in low, reaching for Taylor's legs. Taylor dropped his weight and sprawled, breaking the grip before it formed, then snapped his knee up into the man's face. He could feel cartilage crunch and blood spurted from the man's nose as he stumbled backward, hands flying to his face.

The one in the Carhartt jacket circled right, looking for an opening. Taylor gave him one, deliberately dropping his guard on that side. The man took it, throwing a wide hook aimed at Taylor's head. Taylor slipped inside the punch, trapped the extended arm, and twisted. The joint torqued wrong and the man yelped and tried to pull away, but Taylor held on, using the leverage to spin him into the side of the parked pickup truck. The man's head bounced off the door panel with a hollow bang.

The big one recovered and charged again, this time keeping his hands up, moving like someone who'd been in real fights, but was still just a brawler. He threw a straight right that Taylor blocked, then followed with a left hook to the body. Taylor absorbed it on his forearm, feeling the impact radiate up to his shoulder. Damn, the guy was strong. He countered with a quick jab to the man's throat, pulling it just enough to bruise instead of crush. Unless he had to, killing these guys would make them more of a problem than he wanted them to be. The big man gagged and backed off, coughing.

The one with the broken nose had recovered enough to rejoin the fight, though blood still poured down his chin and soaked into his shirt collar. He came at Taylor from behind, wrapping both arms around Taylor's torso in a bear hug, trying to pin his arms.

Taylor stomped down on the man's instep, grinding his heel into the small bones of the foot. The guy screamed again, and his grip loosened. Taylor drove his head backward, the crown of his skull connecting with the bridge of the already-broken nose. The man howled and let go completely, dropping to his knees on the sidewalk.

The one in the Carhartt jacket pushed off the truck, shaking his head to clear it. He pulled a folding knife from his pocket, flicking it open with his thumb. A four-inch blade, fixed now, held low and ready.

Taylor backed up three steps, creating space, his hand moving to his hip. This took things to another level, but he still didn't draw his gun. Not yet. He didn't have the cover of law enforcement anymore and there was a stink to this whole town that Taylor was sure would mean trouble for him if he did shoot someone.

The man with the knife advanced slowly, keeping the blade between them, moving in small lateral steps. He feinted high, then cut low toward Taylor's midsection. Taylor twisted away, the blade passing six inches from his stomach. The man recovered immediately, resetting his stance, not overextending.

He was good.

The big one had caught his breath and came in from Taylor's left, trying to bracket him. Taylor couldn't watch both at once, not effectively. He needed to end this fast.

The knife came in again, a quick slash aimed at Taylor's forearm. Taylor pulled back, then immediately stepped forward inside the man's guard before he could reset. Taylor caught the knife hand at the wrist with his left hand, controlling it, and drove his right fist into the man's solar plexus. The air went out of the guy in a whoosh. Taylor twisted the wrist, applying pressure to the joint in a direction it wasn't designed to bend. The knife clattered to the pavement. Taylor kicked it away, then shoved the man backward into the big one, tangling them both up.

The one with the broken nose was trying to stand, using the pickup truck for support. Blood covered the lower half of his face and dripped onto the sidewalk in fat drops that looked black in the late afternoon light.

Taylor moved toward him, grabbed a handful of jacket, and yanked him away from the truck. The man swung a weak punch that Taylor blocked with his forearm, then Taylor drove three quick shots into the man's ribs, left-right-left. The man folded, gasping, and Taylor let him drop.

The big one had disentangled himself and squared up again, but the fight had gone out of his eyes. He could see how this was going to end. Still, he came forward, throwing a combination that Taylor deflected and countered, catching him with a right cross that snapped his head to the side. The big man's knees buckled. He didn't go down, but he didn't come forward again either.

The one who'd had the knife was back on his feet, cradling his wrist against his chest. He looked at Taylor, then at his two partners, then back at Taylor.

"Next time," Taylor said. "Bring more guys."

None of them responded. The one with the broken nose stayed on the ground, curled on his side. The big one backed away slowly, hands up in a gesture that wasn't quite surrender but close to it.

The one with the injured wrist just stared, like he wanted to kill Taylor and was angry that he couldn't back it up.

Taylor walked past them to his rental car, watching them in his peripheral vision. None of them moved to follow. He reached his car and stopped, his hand on the door handle, and looked back at them.

The big one shook his head. "You're making a mistake."

"From where I'm standing, it looks like you're the one who made the mistake."

But the big one just turned away, helping the one with the broken nose to his feet. The three of them limped toward a truck parked farther down the street, the one with the injured wrist still cradling it against his body. They climbed in, the engine started, and they pulled away, heading east out of town.

Taylor stood beside his car, watching until they disappeared. His ribs ached where he'd blocked the body shot. His knuckles were scraped and starting to swell. Relatively minor damage, all said and done. He'd had worse from sparring sessions with Whitaker, who fought like she was trying to kill him even in training.

He was glad of it now. Seven years ago, he was like those guys. A brawler. If he'd stayed that way, it would have come down to having to shoot one of them.

He turned to face the street, looking back at the spot where the fight had happened. Blood on the sidewalk. Scuff marks. The knife still lying in the gutter where he'd kicked it.

This was going to be a problem. He could feel the trap.

Taylor looked around, seeing Corky's bar sitting almost caddy-corner to where he was. He gave it another moment's thought and then started walking toward the bar.

Ten minutes later, he was walking back out of the bar and wasn't at all surprised to find a patrol car sitting behind his rental, blocking it in.

Sheriff Brody leaned against the driver's side door of the cruiser, arms crossed over his chest, with Collins standing next to Taylor's car. Taylor kept walking until he stood about ten feet away.

"Mr. Taylor." Brody straightened. "You need to come with us."

"Why?"

"Three men were attacked right in this spot about twenty minutes ago. Two of them are at the hospital right now getting their wounds tended to."

That was a lot of bluster for a fight that took place with witnesses watching out the diner window and blood still on the sidewalk a few feet from where the sheriff was standing.

But if they wanted to play it this way, he could play dumb.

"That so?" he said.

"It is. All three men have filed complaints identifying you as their attacker and saying you assaulted them unprovoked." Brody pulled out a pair of handcuffs from his belt. "You're under arrest."

"Would it matter if I said they attacked me first?"

"That's for the court to figure out. Turn around, hands behind your back."

Taylor didn't move. He kept his eyes on the sheriff, watching both men's body language. Brody wanted this to go smoothly, but Collins clearly wanted Taylor to do something. He was geared up for a fight.

"You're making a mistake," Taylor said.

"We're not the ones who attacked someone," Collins said. "Go ahead and make this harder than it needs to be. See how you like being trussed up and gagged before getting thrown in the back of the car."

Taylor gave him another look, then turned and put his hands behind his back. A moment later, he felt the cold metal on his wrists, followed by their metallic click. Collins squeezed them harder than he needed to before double-locking them, causing the edge of the cuff to cut into his skin.

He certainly was proud of himself, giving a self-satisfactory smile as he guided Taylor toward the cruiser.

Taylor bided his time, bending to get in, just in case Collins thought he could get away with slamming his head into the car door. As soon as he was seated, the door slammed shut and Brody got behind the wheel while Collins took shotgun.

The station was less than five minutes away, and no one talked the whole way. The silence continued as they processed him, taking his phone, wallet, keys, and the Glock he carried in a holster at his back. Brody made a show of logging everything into evidence and telling him the penalty for carrying an unregistered firearm.

Taylor didn't say anything to any of that.

They led him down a short hallway to a cell. Taylor crossed over to a metal bench bolted to the wall as the door clanged shut.

Brody stood outside the bars. "Should've left when you had the chance."

"Probably. Then I wouldn't have been jumped by those guys in the parking lot, trying to take me three to one."

"Funny thing about that." Brody pulled a small notebook from his pocket and flipped it open, making a show of reading. "All three of them say they were walking to the diner when you started the fight. You just rushed at them as soon as you came out of the door. A couple at one of the windows corroborated their description of the event."

"That's bullshit."

"Maybe. Maybe not." Brody closed the notebook. "What I know is I've got five witnesses saying one thing, and you saying another. Do you know how much time you'll serve for aggravated assault? Depending on some of those injuries, the DA might even bump that up to attempted murder. Give you some real time."

"Is that what you're planning on charging me with?"

"We'll see."

"So, not charging me right away. Let me guess, you know your witnesses won't hold up, so you're planning on holding me for forty-eight hours without charging me. Maybe then make a big show of letting me go and saying the charges could still be brought at any time. Probably another threat to leave town thrown on top of that."

"No, smart ass. Here, we like to do a little investigation, make sure we have all the facts before we charge someone."

"Well then, here's a fact for you. There's a security camera mounted above the entrance to Corky's bar that points right at the street. It's got a clear view of that parking lot where those three men attacked me."

"Is that so?"

"It is. Which is why you saw me walking out of there when you came to pick me up. I went into the bar right after the fight and talked to the owner. He was nice enough to pull up the footage for me and it shows the whole thing, which doesn't include me rushing out of the diner and attacking anyone. What it does show is those guys blocking my path and me defending myself, one of them pulling a knife and me defending myself. Very clear who started it."

"That right?"

"Got a copy on my phone. Even emailed it to myself too, just to be safe," Taylor said, watching the sheriff's face. "Just in case my phone somehow disappeared or broke. Already backed up in three different places."

Brody was quiet for a long moment.

"You think you're real smart, don't you?"

"I think any DA who watches that footage will throw out those complaints in about five seconds. And if you try to push this anyway, it's going to look *real* bad."

"Just because you used to be some kind of fed doesn't mean shit to me. We have a procedure to follow and we're going to do it."

"So you figured out who I am then?"

"We do have computers down here, contrary to what you might think."

"Then you know I have friends. People who'll notice if I disappear for two days."

"Is that a threat?"

"Just a statement of fact. Before I came out of that bar, I called my old partner and told her I thought I was about to get picked up on some bullshit charge. Told her about you warning me to leave town and said I figured you might try to hold me for a few days and then let me go."

Taylor hadn't actually thought to do that until just this minute, although he wished he had. If push came to shove, Brody could hold him and it was unlikely anyone would realize he was missing before he got released.

Which would be a massive pain in the ass. Thankfully, Brody was the skittish type. Jumpy.

"You're bluffing."

"Maybe. You want to find out?" Taylor held his stare. "She's got pull. She works major cases and is tasked just under the director himself. If I don't check in with her tonight, she's going to make calls, and once those calls start, you're going to have federal people crawling all over this town asking questions about how you treat visitors. You wouldn't have any reason not to want feds all over your town, would you?"

Brody just scowled and turned, walking away down the hallway.

Five minutes passed, then ten, and Taylor started to wonder if he'd overplayed his hand. If Brody were smarter, he'd take the extra hour, see who Taylor called. Hell, he could even just call the bar owner and ask what Taylor did when he was inside the bar.

Thankfully, Brody wasn't nearly as smart as he thought he was.

Fifteen minutes after Taylor had been walked into the cell, Brody came back with a ring of keys, unlocking it.

"You're free to go."

Taylor stood and walked out without saying a word. They went back to the processing area where his belongings sat in a plastic tray on the counter. He checked everything: phone, wallet, keys.

"My gun, please. I know you saw it was properly registered and permitted. So, unless you want to be talking to a judge about taking away a man's Second Amendment rights, followed by phone calls, and then feds all over town, I'd suggest you give it back."

Brody scowled again and jutted his chin at Collins. He left, coming back a moment later with the weapon. They watched as Taylor clipped it back on his belt, under his jacket.

"You need to leave Glacier Falls. Tonight," Brody said.

"Can't do that."

"Why not?"

"Because Roy Breyer deserves better than what you're giving him. His daughter deserves to know what happened. Deserves to bury her father. I'm not leaving until I get answers."

"Then you're a fool."

"Probably."

Brody stepped closer. Not quite into Taylor's space, but close enough to make the threat implicit.

"Accidents happen to people who don't mind their own business. You've already seen that. Maybe you should think about what happens to people who keep pushing when they're told to stop."

"I have thought about it." Taylor met his eyes. "That's why I'm still here."

The sheriff's face twisted into something between a sneer and a grimace. He wanted to say more, Taylor could see that in his face, but he didn't. He just turned and walked back toward his office.

Taylor looked at Collins, who looked equally pissed, then turned and walked out of the police station.

Chapter 7

Taylor pulled out of the sheriff's office parking lot and drove toward the edge of town, following the directions the cook had given him. Campbell Road was supposed to branch off from the main state road that headed up into the hills, which was at least marked on his map, but that didn't mean it would be easy to find.

In his experience, roads like this were rarely well-marked.

His phone rang as he passed the last few houses on the outskirts of town, the cell towers still providing strong coverage before he'd lose the signal in the mountains.

"Taylor," he said as he answered.

"Mr. Taylor? This is Ellis Watson with the Department of the Interior. Agent Whitaker gave me your number and said you had some questions about activities in your area."

Taylor slowed and pulled into a gravel turnout beside the road, wanting to give the conversation his full attention before he lost cell service.

"That's right. I'm looking into Mountain Vista Industries up here in Glacier Falls, Minnesota. Trying to understand what they're doing exactly."

"One sec," Watson said, and Taylor could hear him tapping away on his keyboard. "Yeah, we've got a file on them. Huh, this is interesting. They filed a patent application about eighteen months ago for some kind of advanced processing system for radioactive materials."

"Radioactive materials?"

"High-level waste processing, according to their documentation. They claim they've developed a method to break down radioactive byproducts from industrial manufacturing, clean them up, and extract valuable materials that can be resold. Supposed to render the waste products inert and harmless. If that works, it would be big."

Taylor watched a pickup truck drive past, heading back toward town with what looked like camping gear in the bed. Probably someone who'd been up in the hills for a few days. "But does it work?"

"Seems to. I have notes here about an inspection where they demonstrated the technology, and both our people and the state regulators were pretty convinced. The science seems solid, at least on paper and in their pilot demonstrations."

"Isn't this a thing for Commerce or the Patent Office? Why was Interior involved in the first place?"

"Water rights and environmental impact. Their process is apparently pretty water-intensive, so they need to pull significant volumes from the Missouri River. But according to their specs, they're putting it back cleaner than when they took it out. Still, anytime someone wants to divert that much water from a major waterway, we have to sign off on it."

"What does 'significant volume' mean?"

"According to the paperwork, a couple million gallons a day during peak operation, which sounds like a lot, but it's not enormous by industrial standards. Still, it is enough that we needed to make sure it wouldn't impact downstream users or the local ecosystem."

"And you were satisfied with their answers?"

Watson paused, and Taylor could hear papers rustling in the background. "Like I said, the technology seemed legitimate. They brought in some heavy-duty engineers and scientists to walk us through the process. MIT-trained chemical engineers, former DOE people, that kind of pedigree. The state environmental agency was involved, too, along with EPA and BLM."

At the mention of BLM, Taylor's mind went back to the newspaper article he'd found about the missing inspector. "You said BLM was part of the review?"

"Sure. There's a land management area up in those hills, plus some old mining claims that fall under federal jurisdiction. Standard procedure when you've got industrial development near federal lands."

"I read something about a missing BLM inspector in the area. You know anything about that?"

"Missing inspector?" Watson's voice carried genuine surprise. "When was this?"

"The article I saw was from about six weeks ago, but it was light on details."

"Hmm. That's not something that would necessarily cross my desk, but ..." More paper rustling. "I don't see anything in our files about a missing federal employee. But if BLM sent someone out to survey the area, it would likely be to assess potential impact on the land management zones from Mountain Vista's operation."

"What kind of impact would they be looking for?"

"Groundwater contamination, air quality, noise pollution, truck traffic on federal access roads. Standard environmental assessment stuff. These big industrial operations can affect a pretty wide area, even when they're on private land."

"But you have nothing on this guy?"

"I'm afraid not. Different department, different jurisdiction. BLM handles its own personnel and survey operations. If someone went missing, it would be an internal matter for them unless it became a law enforcement issue."

"Okay. So the stuff Mountain Vista is working on is on the up and up, though, right?"

"Seems to be. I mean, the technology is pretty cutting-edge, but that's not necessarily unusual. There's a lot of innovation happening in waste processing these days, especially with radioactive materials. The liability and disposal costs for that stuff are so high that there's real money to be made if you can develop better handling methods."

"And you believed their claims about making the waste harmless?"

"The demonstrations were convincing. They showed us samples of processed material that tested clean according to our equipment. But I'll admit we didn't do extensive independent testing. Our role was mainly to evaluate the water usage and environmental impact, not to validate the underlying technology."

"Who would have done that kind of validation?"

"EPA would have looked at the environmental and safety aspects. The Nuclear Regulatory Commission might have been involved if it's handling certain types of radioactive materials. And the state environmental agency would have done its own review."

"But as far as you know, everyone signed off on it?"

"According to this, they did."

"How long ago did this review process happen?"

"Let me check ..." Watson paused. "Looks like the initial application was filed about two years ago, with the final approvals coming through last spring. They've been in the construction phase since then, building out their facility."

"And there haven't been any issues since then? No complaints or follow-up investigations?"

"Nothing that's in the file, though again, once we issue the permits, ongoing monitoring usually falls to state and local authorities unless there's a specific federal concern or a lot of reports of problems in the area."

All of which meant Mountain Vista looked like the real thing, which didn't answer any of Taylor's questions. He knew they were involved, but he couldn't see how they'd be willing to go to these lengths to buy up the land.

They'd already had their inspections and gotten everything passed. True, the BLM guy added more questions, but that might not be tied to them.

"Okay, I think that about covers it. Thanks for the information."

"Sure thing. I owed Whitaker anyway."

"Don't we all," Taylor said, and hung up.

As he pulled the car back onto the road, he started to file the information away. This thing was turning out to be a massive pain in the ass. He had a lot of stuff pointing to something going on, and even a lot of it tied together, but nothing solid.

There was some piece of information he was missing that would explain what was going on. He just needed to find it.

The turn off was about six miles outside of town, just where the cook had said it'd be, the road changing from state-maintained asphalt to gravel, then to little more than two ruts cut through pine and scrub. Taylor's rental bounced over rocks and roots, the suspension working hard, and he kept his speed down because the last thing he needed was a broken axle in the middle of nowhere. The trees closed in on both sides, branches scraping the windows when the ruts forced him too far left or right.

Pete had said the cabin was about three miles past the old mine shaft, which meant Taylor had to watch for the turnoff. The first landmark came up after twenty minutes of slow driving, a rusted gate hanging open on one hinge, and beyond it, the collapsed remains of what might have been a barn. Another mile and he passed a second ruin, this one just foundation stones and a pile of rotted timber that could have been anything.

The road to the mine shaft came up on his left, marked by a barricade that must have been put up twenty years ago with a faded sign that said, 'Mine Closed.'

Or at least, Taylor assumed that was the road to the old mine.

Three more miles and the trees opened up into a clearing. A cabin sat in the center, small and weathered, built from logs that had turned dark gray from years of exposure. A stone chimney rose from the center of the roof, and smoke drifted up from it.

Somebody was home.

A pickup truck that was maybe ten years old, but clean and well-maintained, sat near a woodpile that looked like it could last through two hard winters. Solar panels on poles behind the cabin caught what little light filtered through the overcast sky.

Taylor pulled up next to the truck and cut the engine. He stepped out, and the temperature dropped at least ten degrees from what it had been in town, the altitude and the wind combining to cut through his jacket. He zipped it all the way up and walked toward the cabin, his boots crunching on frozen ground.

The door opened before he reached it.

The man who stepped out was somewhere in his sixties, lean and weathered, with iron-gray hair pulled back in a ponytail and a beard that reached halfway down his chest. He wore canvas work pants and a flannel shirt under a down vest, and he held a rifle in both hands. Not pointed at Taylor, but not exactly pointed away either.

"Help you with something?"

Taylor stopped about fifteen feet from the porch, keeping his hands visible. "I'm looking for Jake Morrison."

"You found him. You got a reason for driving up here?"

"My name's John Taylor. I'm a friend of Roy Breyer."

He looked Taylor up and down one more time and lowered the rifle, leaning it against the doorframe. "Roy's dead."

"I know. That's why I'm here."

Morrison studied him for a long moment, then jerked his head toward the cabin. "Come on in, then. Cold out here."

The interior was sparse but functional. A wood stove in the corner radiated heat; the space held a narrow bed, a small kitchen area with propane appliances, a table with two chairs, and not much else. Books lined a shelf on one wall, and a ham radio setup occupied another corner. Everything was clean and organized, the home of someone who'd learned to live with only what he needed.

Morrison shut the door and moved to the stove, opening it to toss in another log. "Coffee?"

"Sure."

He poured two cups from a pot on the stove and handed one to Taylor. They both sat at the table, and Morrison wrapped his hands around his mug like he was drawing warmth from it.

"How do you know Roy?" Morrison asked.

"He and I served together. After he died, his daughter called me and asked me to come and help her out with some stuff."

Morrison nodded. "I knew he'd been in the service, but he never talked much about it."

"He wouldn't have." Taylor sipped his coffee. It was strong and bitter, the way he liked it. "When's the last time you saw him?"

"A few weeks back. He didn't call ahead or nothing, just showed up one afternoon saying he was looking into some things and wanted to make sure I knew to be careful."

"Careful about what?"

"The water. He said I shouldn't drink from my well anymore, and sure as hell shouldn't drink anything that came from the town supply. Told me to haul water in from outside the county if I could, or at least boil the hell out of anything I pulled from the ground around here."

"He say why?"

"Said he was looking into problems with the water quality in town, thought it might be connected to Mountain Vista." Morrison's eyes went hard when he said the name. "Wouldn't surprise me none if that bunch of bastards were poisoning the whole damn valley."

"You worked for them."

"Long time ago, when they were still Mountain Vista Mining. Spent twenty years underground, breaking my back to pull copper out of the earth so the family could get richer." Morrison pulled up his left sleeve, showing an arm that bent at an odd angle halfway between elbow and wrist. "Cave-in back in 'ought-three. Broke my arm in four places, crushed two vertebrae. Company doctor said I was good to go back to work after six weeks, but I couldn't lift fifty pounds without my back seizing up and couldn't hold a jackhammer without my arm going numb. They kept me on for another month, had me sweeping floors and pushing paper, then let me go. No pension, no compensation beyond what workers' comp paid out, which wasn't much. Forty-two years old and I was done."

"So you don't have much love for them."

"They used me up and threw me away, same as they did to plenty of others. But that was years ago. They closed down most of the mining operations when the veins played out and it wasn't profitable anymore. Then, old man Hutchins retired, handed the company over to his son, who decided to rebrand it into some cockamamie environmental company. Load of horseshit if you ask me."

"Did Roy mention anything specific about what he found?"

"No, he just said he was looking into it, that something wasn't right, told me to be careful with the water and that he'd let me know more when he had it figured out. Guess he didn't get the chance."

Taylor finished his coffee, setting the cup to one side. "You've been up here a while; have you seen anyone else in the hills recently? Someone out of place, maybe?"

"Maybe. I was out hunting about three weeks back, maybe four, and saw a truck parked off one of the old logging roads that cuts past the northern shaft. I think it was a government truck because it had some kind of logo on the door that kind of looked like the type, but I was too far away to make out what it said.

Just saw the colors, blue and white, maybe some red. It was real official-looking."

Taylor felt something click into place. "You get a look at who was driving it?"

"Nope, didn't see anybody. The truck was just sitting there, empty. I thought about walking over to check it out, but I figured if it was government business, I didn't need to be sticking my nose in it, so I headed the other direction and left it alone."

"This was near one of the old mine shafts?"

"Northern shaft, yeah. It's about four miles from here, maybe a little more. They closed it down back in 'ninety-eight, sealed the entrance with concrete and steel. No reason for anybody to be up there unless they were poking around where they shouldn't be."

"The shaft's up high?"

"Yeah, maybe eight hundred feet above the valley floor. The river's down below, running southeast. No roads connecting them, no trails worth mentioning."

Taylor thought about that. A sealed mine shaft high above the river, a government vehicle parked nearby for no apparent reason. There had been a whole range of government people checking out Mountain Vista, according to Watson, but that had been almost a year ago, maybe six months at the latest.

The only other government official up here more recently that Taylor knew of was the missing BLM guy.

"How many old shafts are up in these hills?"

"Half a dozen, maybe more. They dug all through here for almost a hundred years. Most of the shafts are sealed like the northern one, but some of the older ones are just gated with chain-link. Kids used to sneak in before the company put up better fences. You think somebody's using the old mines for something?"

"I don't know yet."

"But you're going to find out."

"That's the plan."

Morrison walked to a drawer and pulled out a folded map. He spread it on the table and pointed to a spot in the hills. "Northern shaft is here. The logging road comes in from the west, curves around and heads back down toward the valley. If you're planning to drive up there, you'll need four-wheel drive and some daylight. Road's rough as hell."

Taylor studied the map, memorizing the location and the approach routes. "Any other way in?"

"You could hike it from the south, come up through the trees. Take you a few hours, but you'd have better cover. You planning to go up there?"

"Probably."

"Then be careful. Those old mines were sealed up like that for a reason. If it's still standing, it's likely to collapse on you as anything else. I'd sure as hell not go in one if I didn't have to."

"I'll keep that in mind," Taylor said, folding the map and handing it back.

Morrison waved it off.

"Keep it. I know these hills well enough I don't need it."

Taylor pocketed the map and stood. "You have a phone up here?"

"Satellite phone. Why?"

"If you see anyone else driving around, anyone who looks like they don't belong, could you call me," Taylor said, handing him one of his security company cards, "and maybe keep close to home for the next week or so."

Morrison frowned. "I guess. You think I'm in danger?"

"I think Roy came up here to warn you for a reason. So yeah, maybe you are."

Morrison nodded to the rifle leaning up against the doorframe. "I can take care of myself."

"I'm sure you can. But if things go sideways, you might need some help."

Morrison considered that, then nodded. "All right. I see anyone, I'll call it in."

Taylor opened the door and stepped out onto the porch. The cold bit at his face immediately, and he zipped his jacket all the way up. Morrison followed him out.

"You find out what happened to Roy, you let me know."

"I will."

Taylor walked to his rental and climbed in. He started the engine and let it idle for a moment, looking back at the cabin.

Morrison stood on the porch, watching him as Taylor put the truck in gear and backed around until he faced the way he'd come. Morrison lifted his free hand in farewell, then turned and went back inside.

It was getting late in the afternoon, and if he didn't want to be walking through the woods in the dark, he needed to get a move on.

Chapter 8

Taylor had to stop a quarter mile before the mine itself. Someone had pulled a gate across the road and locked it with a fairly new-looking lock. Not new new, but if this mine closed down years ago, this lock hadn't been there the whole time. The "No Trespassing" sign, however, probably had, and looked older than the barrier itself. He backed up until he found a pull-off he'd passed earlier. Not even a pull-off, just a flattish area where no trees had grown.

The walk down gave him time to second-guess this. What was he even looking for? While it was pretty certain Mountain Vista was wrapped up in something, it seemed unlikely that he'd find it in an old mine.

However, the BLM guy was definitely connected, and Morrison had seen his truck down here, which meant some part of it was worth looking at.

About two hundred yards past the gate, around a bend and a thick set of trees, was the entrance to the mine. Taylor stopped about thirty feet away, studying it. The wooden framework looked like it had been waiting to collapse for the last fifty years. Support beams tilted at angles, boards hung loose from rusted nails, and the whole structure seemed to sag inward. One of the main crossbeams had a crack running through it that he could see even from here.

It was a death trap.

This was a bad idea. A really bad idea.

But he was here, and this was where he was going to find his answers.

Taylor clicked on his flashlight and approached slowly. Up close, it looked even worse. Gaps between boards where he could see into the darkness beyond. The wood was so rotted in places that it crumbled when he touched it. It was the kind of entrance that screamed "structural failure imminent."

He stepped inside, staying close to the right wall, testing each step before committing his weight. The timbers groaned whenever he touched anything. Somewhere deeper in, he could hear the sound of water dripping.

And then, about a hundred feet past the entrance, everything changed.

The wood was the first thing he noticed. Instead of old, rotting beams that looked like they were going to just crumble into dust, there was treated lumber, dark with preservative. Not fresh from the hardware store, but maintained. Solid. Someone had reinforced this section while letting the entrance rot.

And it hadn't been done recently. This work was maybe a year old, give or take.

Why would anyone care about the structural integrity of an abandoned mine? And why only the interior?

Taylor moved deeper, one hand trailing along the rough stone wall. His light swept across the floor and caught something in the dust: parallel wheel tracks in the dirt floor. They were fairly recent, too. Anything longer than a week or so, and they would have disappeared.

Something heavy had been wheeled in here. Repeatedly, from the look of it.

He followed the tracks.

The tunnel branched twice, but the tracks only went one way. The newer supports continued in that direction, too, and Taylor noticed something else now: the floor had been cleared in this section. No fallen rocks, no debris. Someone was maintaining access to wherever these tracks led.

The air got colder as he went deeper. Damper. He could hear more water now, a steady trickle running down the walls somewhere ahead. The tracks led straight toward the sound.

The tunnel opened into a chamber, and what was in it made Taylor freeze.

The chamber was filled with containers. Large industrial drums, lined up in neat rows, stacked two and three high along the sides across the whole chamber. The kind of fifty-five-gallon drums you saw on the back of trucks, heavy-duty steel with reinforced rims.

Taylor approached slowly. Some were blue, some gray, some that industrial green color. They looked weathered, paint scratched and faded, but intact. Mostly.

Diamond-shaped placards were on the side of each one, the kind mandated for hazardous materials. He was careful not to touch anything as he got close enough to read the symbols.

The first diamond was red, the second blue, and the fourth yellow and black, a bad combination. Flammable, Extreme Health Hazard, and Radioactive.

"Jesus," Taylor said, taking several steps back from them.

Not all were marked that way. Some were identified as Toxic. Others, corrosive. It seemed a mismatch of warnings, which explained why the barrels were slightly different designs and different colors.

These weren't all from the same place, and suddenly everything slotted into place for him. He knew what Mountain Vista was doing.

From what the person at the Department of the Interior had said, and what he'd read, Mountain Vista had developed a reclamation technology for dealing with industrial waste. It was clear now that they had not developed anything.

They simply took millions of dollars to deal with the stuff and then buried it in a cave.

Taylor backed up another step, suddenly aware of how close he was standing to the barrels. How long had these been here? What was leaking out of them?

There were dozens of barrels in this chamber, maybe fifty or sixty.

How much had they made? On this chamber alone, probably hundreds of thousands in disposal fees they'd never actually incurred costs to process. And if they had other sites, other mines, or even other places in this mine, it was a lot more than that.

Taylor looked over the barrels again, although this time more thoroughly.

A streak of rust ran down the side of one, dark reddish-brown. At the base, a small stain on the stone floor, spreading slowly. He checked another barrel. Same thing. Corrosion eating through the steel, the contents seeping out.

It wasn't surprising, with how damp this place was, of course, the barrels would start corroding. These containers weren't meant for long-term storage in a wet environment.

And that was when the next part of the mystery fell into place. The water deep in the mine must flow down toward the river. It was partially fed by runoff from the hills and mountains. The chemicals leaking out of the barrels must be flowing down with it and dumping into the river, where it would slowly dilute.

Of course, not slowly enough to keep people from getting poisoned by this crap.

But the runoff wasn't in a straight line. It would go in offshoots and tributaries all down the hill, percolating through the soil and rock.

Any of the properties along the river would have their groundwater contaminated, and most of those places were like Pete's, running off of wells. That explained his sick animals.

It also explained the seemingly random parcels Mountain Vista had been buying up, scattered across the valley with no obvious pattern. He bet if he looked at a map of the groundwater runoff to the river, it would match up pretty closely with the properties they'd been buying.

They needed to hide what they were doing, and if people on those properties started getting sick, someone might think about the water and have it tested. And that might have inspectors looking for the source of the contamination, so Mountain Vista had to make sure no one was in the path of the runoff.

And with millions of dollars on the line, there was a lot of motivation to do something about the people who wouldn't sell. Or an old soldier who started asking too many questions.

It also explained why a BLM inspector would go missing. If he'd gotten too close to the truth, they couldn't let him get back to where he might tell someone.

No, it all made sense now.

Taylor pulled his phone out to start taking photos, first of the whole lot, and then of enough detail to be able to use this as proof of what Mountain Vista was doing. This was the smoking gun he'd been looking for. Now he needed to document it and then get someone up here to pull all this in and take control of the site so it could be used as evidence.

He'd worked with Whitaker and the FBI long enough to know that, as a private citizen, just snapping some pictures wouldn't hold up in court. There would be chain of custody problems all by themselves that a well-paid lawyer could rip into.

Still, it was a first step just in case the universe did something that made the evidence up and disappear before he could get someone out here.

As if the universe was listening, as soon as he thought that, after only taking one picture, he heard a sound from toward the entrance of the mine. It was faint, mostly blocked by the granite walls, but he was pretty sure it was a vehicle engine. He froze, switching off the flashlight and moving to the Y-junction to see if he could get a better sense of what was happening.

That's when he heard voices coming his way, and then saw the bobbing circle of a flashlight down near the entrance.

Someone was coming.

Taylor moved fast, heading down the other direction at the Y, turning a corner and going just far enough that he couldn't be seen if they happened to shine their lights down that way. He also couldn't help but notice, leaning up against one of the braces, that these hadn't been replaced like those in the other chamber or those in the tunnel back toward the entrance.

"Check the back chamber first," a voice said, coming toward him. "Make sure nothing's out of place before we start loading."

He didn't dare peek out, in case they were looking, but it sounded like more than just two people, although it was hard to tell with how sound bounced around inside these tunnels.

"That guy isn't here," another voice called out, closer to him, maybe at the Y-junction or even a few steps toward him.

Taylor slipped his sidearm out, just in case they decided to do a more thorough search.

"You sure?"

"Yeah, it's clear. Just the drums."

“Well, we’re still supposed to get rid of this stuff. Boss wants it moved tonight before anyone else comes poking around. Let’s get to work.”

Taylor remained frozen as the men moved past his position and down the other side of the Y to where the chamber with the drums was. The sound of footsteps went with them, which he thought meant that maybe all of the men had gone that way.

Thankfully, he saw no lights at the Y-intersection. He could see flashlights bouncing off the wall down the other branch, along with the sound of men cursing and metal scraping as they dealt with heavy barrels.

“Get the hand truck under that one. Jesus, these things weigh a ton,” one voice said.

“Where’s the manifest?”

“Forget the manifest. Just get them loaded.”

Not wanting to get found, and not sure how many men he was dealing with, Taylor hurried as quickly as he could, without giving himself away, down toward the entrance. Once there, he peeked out, trying to carefully see if there was anyone still out here or if they’d all gone into the mine.

Thankfully, these guys weren’t thinking ahead. There was a truck with Mountain Vista on the side of the door, but no one had been left out there in case someone tried to come in behind them or, God forbid, there was a cave-in.

If it had been him, he would have left one guy out here standing guard. Thank God they weren’t as competent.

Taylor hurried out of the mine and across the open area to the trees just beyond, where they went down slope, finding a rocky outcropping just far enough into the trees to make it hard for them to see him but close enough that he could still see them.

Thank goodness he was wearing his brown coat, which would make it easier to disappear into the dead leaves and foliage.

He’d just gotten to cover when someone came out of the mine, stopping to look around like he was trying to see something. Had he made enough noise for them to come investigate?

He hoped not. The last thing he wanted was a search forcing him further away.

Taylor pulled out his phone and switched it to camera mode, zooming in on the mine entrance, taking several photos, making sure to capture the company name clearly.

More men emerged from deeper in the mine, two of them rolling a hand truck loaded with a single barrel. They wore full protective suits, the kind with integrated hoods and face shields. Bright white plastic that covered them from head to toe. Even their hands were encased in thick gloves.

Taylor's stomach turned. He looked down at his own jacket and jeans. How long had he been standing next to those barrels? What might have gotten on him?

A problem for another day, but one that would definitely bug him.

He pushed the worry aside and focused on the scene in front of him. Two more men appeared with another barrel on a hand truck. They maneuvered the drums up a ramp into the truck bed. The process was slow with each barrel being secured before they went back for another.

Taylor counted seven men total, all in protective gear.

He took more photos, documenting each barrel as it was brought out of the mine. The zoom on his phone wasn't great, but it was good enough to show what was happening.

Too bad he couldn't get a clear shot of the warning labels or anything else stamped on the barrels showing where they had come from. From where he was hiding, he could only see a variety of multicolored barrels coming out of a boarded-up mine.

Twenty minutes passed, then thirty as the men continued to load barrel after barrel from the mine into the truck. After it seemed like every barrel had been moved, although Taylor hadn't gotten a count when he was in the mine, one man walked to the truck cab and returned with a large black case and another followed with what looked like coils of wire.

They set everything down near the mine entrance and opened the case. Taylor couldn't see exactly what was inside from his angle, but he'd seen enough people work with explosives in his day to know what they were doing.

The two men worked on setting the charges while the others moved the truck away, almost out to the road, and began strapping everything down. The men by the mine placed what were almost certainly demolition charges at points along the entrance framing, running det cord between them. Mountain Vista had been a mining company before it turned to this straight criminal enterprise, so it wasn't surprising they'd have charges and det cord, both of which were common in the industry. It also gave another reason why they hadn't repaired the support beams at the front of the mine. After the blast, the wood in the rubble would be old.

The whole thing would look like a natural cave-in, the kind of thing that must happen often with these old mines.

Anyone investigating would see the collapsed entrance and assume the tunnel had simply failed with age and probably wouldn't bother to dig deeper, although he watched them carry charges into the mine itself, so they might be planning on collapsing the mine all the way to the chamber where the barrels had been stored, just to be safe.

It would be all but impossible to pull any evidence out of this place.

The last barrel was secured in the truck. One of the men checked the explosive setup one final time, then jogged back toward the truck, moving faster now that the work was done.

Taylor still had his phone up. He hadn't recorded the whole thing; his phone wouldn't have enough storage for that, but he'd recorded enough to make it clear what they were doing.

The other man stayed near the entrance, clearly holding the detonator. He looked around one last time, confirming everyone was clear, and pressed the switch.

The explosion wasn't as loud as it would have been if all the explosive was out in the open. Not that it was quiet. Most of it was muffled inside the mine, just a series of cracks and a deep rumble. The mine entrance collapsed inward, timber and rock falling together in a cascade of debris, and dust billowed out in a gray cloud, spreading through the clearing. The sound rolled through the hills, startling birds from nearby trees.

When the dust began to settle, nothing remained of the entrance except a slope of broken rock and splintered wood. It looked exactly like what it was supposed to look like, an old mine that had finally given up and sealed itself.

The man with the detonator walked to the truck and climbed in. The vehicle pulled forward, turning onto the dirt road, moving out of sight. Taylor kept recording until it disappeared around the first curve.

He lowered the phone and stared at the collapsed mine entrance. The photos and video he'd captured were something, but they weren't enough. A truck with Mountain Vista's name on it near an old mine wasn't proof of illegal dumping. Men in protective gear could have been doing legitimate cleanup work, since this property almost certainly still belonged to the company. The barrels in his photos didn't show their contents clearly enough to prove what was inside them or that these guys hadn't brought them empty into the mine.

And none of it would pass chain of custody if it was used in a court case.

He'd lost his smoking gun and still needed something that directly connected Mountain Vista to the deaths, to the contamination, and to the cover-up. Without that, the company could claim they were simply doing remediation work at old mine sites.

Taylor stood and brushed dirt from his jeans. His legs protested after being in a crouch for so long, his muscles stiff and sore. He worked his way back through the woods toward where he'd left the rental car, taking a longer route to stay out of sight in case anyone was watching the road.

When he reached the car, he climbed into the driver's seat and started the engine, letting it warm while he pulled out his phone.

The photos looked decent, all things considered. A clear, if dark, shot of the cavern with all the barrels and video of the explosion and the collapse.

Not enough.

Taylor put the car in gear and pulled onto the dirt road, heading back toward town.

At least he had answers. He knew why Mountain Vista was buying up the land and that they were killing people to keep their real crime a secret. The motive was easy: money.

Mountain Vista was making millions from disposal fees they never spent on actual disposal. Anyone who threatened that operation, whether it was someone whose property would be tainted by chemical runoff, a federal inspector or an old soldier who asked too many questions, they got rid of and called it an accident, thanks to the sheriff and doctor being in their pocket.

The sun was going down when he got back to the state road. He still had the tour of the facility the next morning. It was unlikely they'd show him anything incriminating, but they didn't know he knew what was going on, and it might give him something. Some evidence he could hand to Whitaker. The death of the BLM inspector was enough to make this federal, but he needed enough for her to be able to open an investigation.

He just had to find it.

Chapter 9

Taylor drove back up the mountain road, his rental car bouncing over ruts and washboard sections that hadn't improved since his first trip up earlier that day. Mountain Vista had moved fast. He knew they were keeping an eye on him, but even they didn't know he was coming to the mine, which meant they were being careful, taking precautions. But they were doing so quickly, not being careful. That bothered him less than it should have. People who moved that fast made mistakes.

He pulled up to Morrison's cabin and killed the engine. Morrison appeared in the doorway before Taylor could get out of the car, rifle in hand but pointed at the ground.

Taylor climbed out of the car and started toward him.

"Back already," Morrison said.

"Hit a dead end."

Morrison gave him a look and then gestured him inside, saying, "Come on in."

Morrison led him in, poured two cups of coffee from the pot on the stove and handed one over.

"So?" Morrison said.

Taylor sat at the table. "Found what I was looking for, but Mountain Vista got there before I could do anything. Cleaned everything out, covered their tracks."

"That's what they do. Always cover everything up. Gotta make sure the company survives. What did you find?"

"I found the mine and it was as advertised, or so it seemed at first. Abandoned, looking like it was going to fall down any second, but once I got through the entrance, all that changed. It was reinforced, recently."

"Really? Why in the hell would they do that?"

"Because they were using it again, but not for mining. They were storing dozens of industrial drums filled with hazardous waste, from the looks of it, and making room for what looked like more."

"What do you mean, hazardous?"

"Looked like a mix of different stuff, but all nasty. Radioactive material, toxic chemicals, corrosive substances, you name it. Most of it looked industrial, like by-products or something."

"Those sons of bitches."

"No kidding. I think it's tied to this revolutionary process they announced for breaking down toxic waste, reclaiming industrial waste. Except the process isn't a process at all, it's a scam. They're just burying the waste in the old mine shafts. Worse, the barrels were rusting. Some of them already started leaking. All of that contamination seeps into the groundwater, flows down into the river. That's why they've been buying up all the riverfront property. They're not worried about water rights for their fake processing system, they're trying to control who can test the water downstream."

"And Roy figured this out."

"I think so, and I think it's what got him killed."

"So you call up the feds or whoever, show them the mine. That shit has to be illegal."

"That was the plan, but like I said, they're cleaning up their tracks. They know I'm poking around and they're playing it safe. While I was there, a truck came in, they loaded up the barrels and collapsed the mine."

"Damn," Morrison said. "My land. My water. Everything I've got left in this world, and these bastards are poisoning it right under my feet. I can't even sell this place and get out. Who's going to buy property with contaminated groundwater? Everything I've worked for, everything I've got to show for sixty-three years on this earth, and it's all worthless now. Should have gotten some kind of insurance, although they're just as evil. Probably would tell me it was an act of God or something and screw me over too."

"Say that again," Taylor said, something clicking for him.

Morrison frowned. "Say what?"

"About insurance."

"I said insurance won't cover it. Why?"

"Because you're right. Insurance companies don't pay out without documentation. They require proof. Death certificates. Autopsy reports. Official findings from the county coroner."

"So?"

"So all those accidental deaths, those people all had families. Those families would have filed life insurance claims. The insurance companies would have required official documentation before they paid out. Doc Henley would have had to sign off on every single one of those death certificates. He would have had to write reports, file paperwork, provide medical findings that supported the accidental death rulings. Sure, he ruled them as accidents, but I bet it wouldn't be hard to disprove some of those autopsies. Henley's a nervous man. With enough pressure, I could get him to talk to the feds. He has to know at least about the murders, since he's covering them up. Once we have him, the rest will come falling down."

"Are you sure about that?"

Taylor was already up, heading for the door and stepping out onto the porch.

"What other choice do I have?" Taylor asked. "I need some kind of evidence, and the odds are I won't just stumble onto another cache of the stuff. That was dumb luck."

Morrison followed him to the door. "What do you want me to do?"

"Stay here and be careful. They know you're up here, and who knows what they're willing to do to cover their tracks. If you see anyone on your property, anyone at all, call me immediately. Don't try to handle it yourself."

"I'm not afraid of them."

"I know. But I need you *alive*. You saw the government truck up here and can at least tie it together with the activity at the mine. They might have taken the barrels and collapsed the mine, but the FBI forensic guys are good, and they have the resources to dig the whole thing up. Put that with what I saw, the few pictures I got, and what you saw, and it gives us some circumstantial evidence. Not enough to stand on its own, but with this kind of thing, we need everything we can get."

"You think they'll come for me?"

"I don't know, but Roy and six other people are dead. These aren't amateurs, and they're not going to stop just because someone's asking questions." Taylor said as he descended the steps and walked toward his car. "I'll call you tomorrow after I talk to Henley."

"And if he still won't cooperate?"

Taylor opened the car door and looked back at Morrison. The older man stood on the porch, backlit by the dim light from inside the cabin.

"Then I'll find something else," Taylor said.

He climbed into the car and started the engine. Morrison remained on the porch, watching as Taylor backed down the narrow drive and turned onto the rutted road that led back toward town.

The drive took longer in the fading light. Taylor's mind examined the angles, working the problem. He still had the tour tomorrow, not that he thought that was going to give him anything actionable. He was going to go, because what the hell. He might find something, but Henley was the key.

He was sure of it. He was neck deep in the entire thing but, seeing how nervous he'd been, Taylor didn't think he was a willing participant. Or at least not an enthusiastic one. He was more like a trapped animal, ready to break.

Taylor just had to give him a little push.

He was almost to the hotel when he reached for the phone. It was getting late in DC, almost ten, which meant that while Whitaker was almost certainly home, Grace had probably already been put to bed, and he'd missed his opportunity.

She picked up on the second ring. "Hey. You missed her. She's already asleep."

"Yeah, I figured. I think I may have broken this thing open, which is why I'm calling. I need a favor."

Silence on the other end. He knew that pause. Things were still tense between them, and he'd already called in one, so a second one was pushing it.

"What kind of favor?"

"The kind that uses FBI resources for something that isn't officially an FBI case."

"Taylor."

"But I know what they're doing, and it's prosecutable. Well, maybe."

"What do you mean, maybe? And what are they doing?"

Taylor heard the exhaustion in her voice. "Mountain Vista isn't developing any revolutionary waste processing technology. They're taking large sums of federal money to dispose of toxic and radioactive waste, then burying it in abandoned mine shafts up in the hills. No processing, no reclamation, just straight-up dumping."

"You're sure about this?"

"I found one of their sites, an old mine shaft that they used to run when they were Mountain Vista Mining, about four miles from the nearest town access. The mine entrance looked abandoned, rotting timber, ready to collapse, but once you got past that facade, the interior was reinforced. New supports, cleared floor, wheel tracks in the dirt. They had at least fifty industrial drums stored in a chamber, all marked with hazmat placards, rusting and leaking. All that contamination was seeping into the groundwater and flowing down into the river, which explains why they've been systematically buying up every piece of riverfront property they can get their hands on and getting rid of anyone who wouldn't sell."

"To control who can test the water."

"Exactly. If people living downstream start getting sick and test their wells, it would raise suspicions. There would be investigations, and someone would figure it out. Mountain Vista needs to own or control every property in the contamination path."

"What kind of proof do you have?" she asked, starting to sound excited.

This was the kind of thing she lived for. Actionable, prosecutable cases. And he was about to let her down.

"I started to take pictures, but a bunch of guys showed up and I had to hide. I only got a couple of pics of the cavern with the barrels, but you can't make out where it is or anything on the drums. They apparently had instructions to remove all of the drums, and then they collapsed the mine entrance with explosives. Thankfully, I got out of there before they caved it in."

"I assume they didn't know you were there?"

"No, I was already under cover when they arrived. I got video of them loading the truck, setting the charges, bringing the mine down, but you can't really see enough. They could be doing anything, and the chain of custody is completely compromised since I was trespassing on private property without a warrant. Any lawyer would tear it apart."

"Send me what you have. I'll look at it."

"I will, but you're not going to get sign-off on this yet, which is why I'm calling."

"So what do you need to get the evidence?"

"I need to check something through the insurance companies. The town doctor, who's also the coroner, is holding onto the autopsies tight, but he would have had to supply some of them to the insurance companies. My thought is, if we could get those, and get one of the families to sign off on exhuming their family member, we can prove the autopsy report was wrong. Insurance fraud with some families out of state would be enough to put it in your jurisdiction and be actionable."

"You think the doctor will fold?"

"He will," Taylor said. "The man was terrified. He wouldn't tell me what kind of accident killed Roy, wouldn't release the body, kept saying he was following the sheriff's orders. He's not a criminal mastermind. He's a small-town doctor who got in over his head and now he's trapped."

"That's assuming he knows enough to be useful."

"He knows about the murders. He had to falsify the autopsy reports for at least some of them. The way he was acting, he knew he was lying, and if he knew he was lying on the autopsies, he would have seen enough to know they were murdered. He'll be the weak link."

"So we've got a corrupt sheriff, a complicit coroner, fraud, and large-scale environmental crimes."

"Plus conspiracy to commit murder, obstruction of justice, and probably a dozen other charges. Also, there's a missing federal agent, although without a body, there's not much I can do with that yet. We just need one of the dominoes to fall, and the rest will come down with it."

"I'll make some calls in the morning. See what I can do about getting an investigation opened."

"You're not going to get approval. Especially once they hear your source is me. Not without something more solid than I have."

"I know, but I can at least try."

"I appreciate it. But while you're doing that, I need to know who those insurance claims were filed with. I could call the families, but I only have contact information for a few, and I don't really have any kind of connection with any of them. If Mountain Vista has already started covering things up, I don't have time to dig for that."

"Alright, I'll see what I can do. What are you going to do while you wait for me to get it?"

"I've been invited on a tour of the Mountain Vista facility tomorrow morning. I ran into the CEO, Wade Hutchins, and he recognized me from some of the old press clippings, of all things, and invited me personally. He knew I was in town and looking into things, and for this to all work, he has to be in bed with the sheriff and the doctor, at the very least. Considering how hard the sheriff has worked to get rid of me, it would be wildly unlikely he didn't know what I was doing."

"Then why invite you?"

"I'm guessing to throw me off the scent, maybe see what I know. He's started to clean house, but it's not like he can store that stuff in his facility. The only way this whole scheme works is if he can make the waste disappear, which means it has to go back in the mines. He wants to find out how long to wait until he can put it back, is my guess."

"Or he's planning on getting rid of you like he did the others."

"Maybe, but he strikes me as clever. Clever enough to know that mine would be a higher profile death if he was able to do it. He doesn't want that kind of eyes on him."

"That's a risky assumption."

"Just a guess, I'm not ruling out him trying something. I'll be ready."

"Just remember you don't have backup this time."

"I know. I'll be careful."

"Okay. I'll call you when I have something."

Taylor arrived at the Mountain Vista facility at nine the next morning. The place sat at the end of a newly paved access road, all clean lines and modern architecture that looked out of place against the rural backdrop. A chain-link fence topped with razor wire surrounded the property, and a guard shack controlled the only entrance. The guard checked his ID against a list and waved him through after making a phone call.

Wade Hutchins met him in the parking lot, well-dressed in slacks and a button-down shirt with the sleeves rolled to his elbows, extending a hand as Taylor climbed out of the rental. His handshake was firm without being aggressive, and his smile reached his eyes in a way that suggested he had practiced it.

"Mr. Taylor, glad you could make it. I have to admit, when I saw you yesterday, I couldn't believe my luck. Not every day you run into someone with your background in a place like Glacier Falls."

"Just visiting an old friend's family."

Of course, Wade had sent those men to clear out the cache in the mine, which meant he knew exactly why Taylor was in town and what he was doing.

Everyone was putting up fronts. Although he had to admit, Hutchins was exceptional at his. If Taylor didn't know he was full of it, he might even be fooled. Of course, Taylor's dislike of anyone a little too smooth, especially after having dealt with politicians the last few years, meant he might not have been fooled either.

"Of course, of course. I remember hearing that Roy was a veteran. I'm guessing that's how you knew him. I didn't know him well, although in a town as small as this, 'not well' is still a hell of a lot better than people know each other in the city. He was a good man. Rock solid. The kind of neighbor you'd want." Wade gestured toward the main building. "Come on, let me show you what we're doing here. I think you'll find it fascinating."

Taylor followed him toward the entrance, taking in the layout as they walked. The main structure was a large warehouse-style building with several smaller outbuildings arranged in a loose semicircle. Heavy-duty trucks were parked in a staging area to the left, and he could see loading bays along the side of the main building. Everything looked new, purpose-built, and expensive.

"We broke ground about eighteen months ago," Wade said, holding the door open. "Got the permits finalized, funding secured, and started construction. Full operations began about six months ago, though we're still in the certification phase."

The interior was climate-controlled, a welcome change from the March cold outside. Wade led him through a reception area and into the main facility floor. The space opened up into a cavernous warehouse filled with machinery, pipes, and industrial equipment. There was a distinct smell, sort of a chemical tang mixed with something metallic and the faint scent of chlorine.

"This is our primary processing floor. What you're looking at is the most advanced waste remediation system in the country, maybe in the world."

Taylor noted the tanks, the network of pipes overhead, the control panels with their blinking lights and digital readouts. It all looked impressive and legitimate, which was exactly the problem. Wade had built a convincing stage set.

"How does it work?"

"The basic principle is filtration and chemical breakdown at the molecular level." Wade walked toward a bank of large steel tanks, each one marked with technical specifications and warning labels. "We take in high-level radioactive, corrosive, and toxic waste, primarily spent fuel rods and contaminated materials from decommissioned reactors, but also industrial by-products from various factories around the nation. The waste arrives in specialized containers, gets logged and cataloged, then moves into the processing stream."

He gestured to a series of smaller tanks connected by pipes. "First stage is separation. We use a proprietary solvent to break down the waste into its component parts. Any radioactive elements, or any other elements that are, on their own, hazardous to people, get isolated, and the inert materials are filtered out.

Second stage is neutralization. We separate out the elements and bombard the components with a specific spectrum of electromagnetic radiation that disrupts their atomic structure, essentially rendering them inert."

Taylor moved closer to examine the equipment, keeping his expression neutral and mildly interested. The setup was elaborate, and he suspected some of it actually functioned, at least enough to pass inspections.

"I've heard you guys are using a lot of water?"

"That's the genius of the system. The whole process is water-based, which makes it incredibly efficient." Wade led him to another section where massive pipes ran from the ceiling down into what looked like filtration systems. "We pull directly from the river. The water acts as both a coolant and a transport medium. After it's been through the system, it gets filtered and treated until it's cleaner than when we took it in. Then it goes back into the river, along with now cleaned water from the shipments we took in. We're actually putting back more water than we take out."

"Cleaned, though, I guess."

"That's right. We're not just avoiding environmental damage, we're actively improving the watershed." Wade's enthusiasm seemed genuine, which made him either a true believer in his own con or a better actor than Taylor had given him credit for. "Every gallon we return is tested and certified. We've got documentation on everything."

"What kind of volume are you processing?"

"Right now, we're at about thirty percent of our projected capacity. We've processed roughly two hundred tons of waste since operations began, with another five hundred tons contracted over the next two years. The federal government's our biggest client, but we're also working with three private utilities and two research facilities. Once we get full certification, those numbers will triple."

"And what would happen if something went wrong? If the waste wasn't actually being neutralized and you were just dumping contaminated water back into the river?"

Wade's expression didn't change, but Taylor caught the slight pause before he answered, the subtle shift in his posture that suggested he was trying to figure out what Taylor was really asking.

"That would be catastrophic. We're talking about heavy metals, radioactive isotopes, chemical toxins. If that got into the groundwater and river system untreated, you'd see contamination spread for hundreds of miles downstream. Cancer rates would spike, birth defects, long-term environmental damage that would take decades to remediate, if it could be remediated at all."

"Expensive cleanup."

"Beyond expensive. We're talking billions of dollars and whole communities permanently affected. But it's not just the money, it's the cost to human life. I got into this to change my family's legacy. To start helping people, which is why we've built in multiple redundancies and safety systems. Every stage of the process gets monitored and tested. We've got sensors throughout the facility that would shut everything down at the first sign of a problem. And we're using the same water source for everything here, the break room, the bathrooms, the drinking fountains. If something was wrong, we'd poison ourselves first."

It was a good answer, or it would have been if Taylor didn't know it was all bullshit.

"Who does your independent testing?"

"We've got contracts with three separate labs, all certified and bonded. They rotate monthly so there's no chance of anyone getting too familiar or cutting corners. Plus, the federal regulators do their own spot checks." Wade gestured back toward the entrance. "Come on, let me show you the intake area."

They moved through a set of heavy doors into a section that looked more like a loading dock. Several bays were empty, but one had a large transport container sitting on a specialized trailer. Workers in protective gear were using a crane system to position the container near what looked like an airlock.

Taylor didn't recognize any of them from the mine cleanup or the guys who jumped him, who Taylor was now certain had been Mountain Vista employees. Which meant they had a lot more people working here than he realized.

He couldn't help but wonder how many knew this was all a sham, and how many were kept on the job so they could say they were doing the job, without actually doing anything but pushing buttons.

"This is where everything comes in. Waste arrives in DOT-approved containers, gets scanned and verified, then moved into the processing area through those airlocks. Nothing enters or leaves without going through decontamination protocols."

The setup was thorough, Taylor had to give him that. If someone came in for an inspection, they'd see exactly what they were supposed to see: a functioning facility that followed every regulation and safety standard.

"When do you expect to get full certification?"

"We're hoping for this year, late summer or early fall. There's a final round of inspections scheduled for June, and assuming everything checks out, we should have it wrapped up by August. You certainly do have some good questions. You should consider a job as a federal inspector."

Taylor let a slight smile show. "Not me. I've done my time with the government. I guess old habits just die hard. It's impressive what you've built here."

"I appreciate that. It's been a long road, a lot of capital investment, a lot of regulatory hoops to jump through. But the technology works, and once we're fully operational, we'll be able to make a real difference. This country's been sitting on radioactive waste for decades with no good solution. We're finally offering one."

Wade walked him around a little bit more, showing him the computerized control room, sampling room for checking the end product, break rooms, and all the other stuff a factory like this would have.

"Thanks for the tour," Taylor said as they headed back out to the parking lot. "It's impressive what you've built here."

"My pleasure. Like I said, it's not every day I get to show it off to someone with your background. So how long are you planning to stick around Glacier Falls?"

"Haven't decided yet. Depends on how things go with Roy's family, probably until the funeral, though."

"Well, if you need anything while you're here, feel free to reach out. Small town, everyone knows everyone, and I like to think I can help people find what they need."

They shook hands again in the parking lot, and Taylor got into his rental while Wade stood watching, still wearing that practiced smile.

Taylor started the engine and pulled out of the parking lot. He couldn't help but think that last question was what Hutchins really wanted to know. He was trying to figure out when they would get the thorn out of their side and could get back to business.

If Taylor had to guess, Roy's body would soon be released for burial. Not that that would actually send Taylor away now. He had his hooks in this thing and would see it through.

He looked in the rearview mirror as he was going through security and saw Wade still standing there, phone already pressed to his ear.

Chapter 10

Taylor pulled out of the Mountain Vista parking lot and headed back toward town. Hutchins had put on a good show, he had to give the man that, and it would have probably fooled him if he didn't already know the truth.

Unfortunately for Hutchins, he did. Now he just had to figure out how to make use of what he knew.

He checked his phone as he was driving and saw a message from Whitaker. She'd gotten him the information he'd asked for.

Checked insurance. Half went through Great Plains Mutual. Sending contact info.

A second text followed with a phone number and the name of the regional office in Sioux Falls.

Taylor pulled over at the intersection with the main highway and dialed the number. The line rang twice before a recorded voice kicked in, walking him through a menu of options. He pressed the number for claims investigation and waited.

"Claims division, this is Rebecca."

"I need to speak with whoever handles your regional investigations for Minnesota and the surrounding states."

"What is this regarding?"

"A possible criminal probe."

There was a pause. "Hold, please."

Taylor had left it vague enough that he hoped they would assume he was with an agency and looking into fraudulent claims. He found that most people just took what they wanted something to mean and ran with it, never questioning what you were actually saying. The line was silent for about thirty seconds, then clicked back to life.

"This is Paige Watson."

Her voice was clear and professional, with just enough edge to suggest that she did not waste time on nonsense.

"Ms. Watson, I am looking into a series of deaths in Glacier Falls, Minnesota, and I understand several of the deceased had policies through Great Plains Mutual."

"Who am I speaking with?"

Taylor kept his phrasing careful. "My name is Taylor. I got your number from Agent Whitaker at the main office in DC. I don't know if she called ahead or not."

Again, everything he said was true, and it was up to her to take that how he meant it or not.

"We did not receive any notification," she said, although something in her voice said that he had her. The caution had been replaced by a professional interest. "How many claims are you looking at?"

"I know three that went through your company: Justin Bradley, Thomas Evans, and Sarah Miller, out of the six accidental deaths in the city in the last eighteen months, and all signed off on by the same doctor."

"Would that be Doctor David Henley?"

"You know him?"

"I know his billing practices, and I'm glad someone finally took my notices seriously. I have been flagging those claims for review for months. No one wants to hear it because there is no proof of actual fraud, but something is not right about the way he documents these cases."

"Was it the number of cases that got your notice?" Taylor asked.

"Yes, that and the toxicology panels. Doctor Henley orders full tox screens on every single case, even when the listed cause of death is obvious. Things like car crashes, falls, and drowning shouldn't need that kind of screen, but he bills for comprehensive blood work anyway."

"I take it that is unusual?"

"It is. It is expensive and completely inappropriate for most accident investigations. We deny that part of the claim, and it is up to him to bill the family, which happens more often than you'd think. It is a way to pad the bill and put more cost on a grieving family, although my guess is he hopes that no one looks at it and just signs off. I am ashamed to say that is what our department did before the second one came in and it got flagged and kicked to my desk."

"What kinds of things are they looking for on these tests? Isn't it common to screen every patient?"

"Basic blood work is done, sure, but Henley orders panels that test for everything. Heavy metals, industrial chemicals, environmental contaminants. That kind of stuff wouldn't be screened for unless there was a suspicion that the death had been caused by some kind of poison or contamination. And even in that case, it is usually requested as a one-off as part of building a case against someone."

Taylor's mind started connecting pieces. "How much does that kind of testing cost?"

"Depends on the specific panel, but we are talking several thousand dollars per case for each test. It adds up fast, especially when you're doing it repeatedly. The problem is, I can't prove he's billing the families for it, after we do the test, and if he is eating the costs, then it is hard to prove fraud."

"Did you see the actual results? The toxicology reports?"

"No, I would only see them if we take it to trial. It is privileged medical information. I can see what was billed and what tests were ordered, the actual findings are confidential, but I am pretty confident something is off here. Three requests from such a small region in such a short amount of time. There is no chance."

She was right, it stank, but she had the motivation wrong. It took Taylor a second, but there was only one reason why he would be ordering toxicology tests for deaths he knew for a fact were not poisonings, and it was not to commit insurance fraud. He was deep enough in this thing to know why they were killing people and that some of those toxins had already gone into the groundwater.

He was building evidence for what was really happening here with the one piece of the operation he had his hands on.

But why? Weren't they his partners?

Or maybe he was not so willing. Henley had struck him as the nervous type. Not the kind of man to get wrapped up in a conspiracy on his own; he would be a wreck the whole time. But very much the kind of guy who could get strong-armed into going along with something.

Henley was not stupid, though. He knew this was risky. He was building an insurance policy. It was not a get-out-of-jail-free kind of proof, since the levels had to be low enough not to be exactly a smoking gun, but it was the kind of thing Hutchins would not want out there.

"Ms. Watson, I need you to send me everything you have. Nothing privileged, of course, but even a list of the screens that were ordered would be enough."

"Will that help you get this guy?"

"Directly, probably not. For that, we will have to get a court order to unseal the records, but it might be enough to use as leverage to get him to talk on his own. It will be faster, at least."

She was quiet for a moment, and Taylor was worried she might say no. These might not be records that legally were required to be kept private, but a big corporation could throw up enough walls to keep the release of any documentation to make this a dead end.

Thankfully, she finally said, "Yeah, I can do that. Give me a few hours to send you something. Just get this guy. People like this piss me off. Where do you want me to send them?"

"That is the plan," Taylor said, gave her his email address, and hung up.

That went better than expected. Half the time, these people were difficult just to be difficult, but Henley had already raised enough red flags and with his request, they were looking into it themselves, so this was just an offer to make her job a little easier.

Taylor turned the car and headed back to the hotel since he wouldn't be able to go over all this on his phone. As soon as he got in, he opened up his laptop at his motel room's desk. The email the agent promised was sitting in his inbox.

There were four attachments and a short line from Paige Watson.

Per our conversation. Billing statements and test orders for all flagged claims. Let me know if you need anything else.

He downloaded the files and opened the first one, which turned out to be a scanned billing sheet filled with columns of text in small print.

Provider: David Henley, M.D. Facility: Glacier Falls Family Clinic. Payer: Great Plains Mutual.

Below that, the meat of it. Date of service. Panel codes. A case reference number. No patient names, just initials and numbers, but it had the dates of each of the orders, and they corresponded roughly with the dates of each of the "accidents."

The pattern wasn't hard to see.

There were some extra tests mixed in, probably legitimate tests ordered for patients in town. He went line by line through the billing sheets and matched them up with the deaths; he only had to make a column of case numbers beside the names.

Each sheet also listed the outside lab that had run the toxicology panels. Most of them went through the same place in Sioux Falls called Plains Regional Diagnostics. A quick search told him that they were the largest medical screening company in the Midwest, which made sense why so many orders had gone through them, and made their information fairly easy to find.

It also had the codes for the tests that had been ordered, which tracked back, on one of the other billing sheets, to something called a comprehensive tox screen, and all of the people killed to hide Mountain Vista's secret had one of those. Helpfully, none of the other people he ordered tests for did, which just further confirmed he had the right grouping.

What it didn't have was what that actually covered or what the test found. Taylor leaned back and thought for a second, walking through his options before finally pulling out his phone and texting Lopez.

Need something. Can you make an email address that looks like it's from someone else? Specifically, a doctor's office in the Midwest?

He hit send and got up to stretch. He already had a good guess what Henley was up to, but he needed something solid he could show the good doctor to force him to cooperate. Anything else, and he might think any threats to turn it over to his conspirators were a bluff, which it was, since Taylor wanted to put them all in jail, not get rid of their weakest member.

Which they certainly would do when they found out Henley was putting together a backup plan.

His phone dinged.

Send me his real address.

Taylor dug the clinic's card out of his wallet and sent that over.

Another message buzzed his phone a few minutes later.

Use: records@gfclinic.net. Anything they send there will bounce straight to you. Should work fine.

"Plains Regional Diagnostics, client services. This is Karen."

"This is Mark from Doctor Henley's office in Glacier Falls," Taylor said, flattening his vowels and slowing his words, trying to match what he'd heard in town. "We had a server crash last night and lost part of our lab interface. Doctor Henley is in chart review and can't see several toxicology reports he signed off on. He needs them back in front of him today."

He heard the light tap of keys on her end.

"Sure, we can resend reports we have on file, but I need to verify the account first. Do you have your client ID and NPI?"

He checked the billing sheet on the bed beside him and found them in the lower right-hand corner of the sheet. There was a light tapping of keys.

"Okay, I have you. Doctor David Henley, Glacier Falls Clinic. Is the information still what we have on file?"

"That's my other problem. The main clinic inbox is tied to the crashed server and we can't access anything on it. Can you send them to records@gfclinic.net?"

"That's not the address I have on file, and I can't send them to a different address that's unverified, not with patient records. I could messenger them over."

"How long will that take?" Taylor asked, hoping it wasn't something fast.

"Two days, probably. Sometimes three."

"Damn," Taylor said, trying to sound disappointed. "He needs them today and it's my ass if I can't get them."

"I'm sorry," she said, her helpful tone vanishing. "But I can't change the delivery address for protected health information just because someone calls and says their system is down. If I start sending results to addresses that aren't on the original orders, that is a HIPAA violation waiting to happen."

"You are not changing anything," Taylor said. He let some strain into his voice. "You are sending them to the ordering provider.

Doctor Henley's direct account is in your system, same domain, same clinic. The only difference is you would be sending them to an email that's working and that we can get into in that black hole of a server. If I could access our original email server, we wouldn't even be having this call, but the doctor needs those records in front of him today and he is not going to wait on IT to rebuild the whole system. Come on, can't you help me out?"

"I'm sorry, but I can't. If the doctor wants to submit new client information through proper channels, we can get the account updated and send it over to anywhere you want, but not until it goes through the proper procedure."

"And how long does that take?"

"A couple ..."

"... of days," Taylor finished, glad again it wasn't an instant process. He was pushing his luck, but this woman was a problem, and he needed to push her to want him off the phone as fast as possible. "Look, the doctor is going to walk out of an exam room soon and he's going to want those charts in his hand and after he's done chewing me out, you are going to get a call from a very upset doctor asking why his lab can't get him his own results. He is already behind on signoffs from last week."

"I'd love to help," she said, sounding like she'd love nothing of the sort. "But there are rules. We can't just send patient data out to anyone who asks."

"I'm not just anyone who asks; you've already verified I am calling from his office. I've verified his client ID and his NPI. I confirmed all of it and the email I'm giving you is even on the same domain as our regular one, which means it's for the same business."

"I can't ..."

"Look, I know you have policies you have to follow, and you need to stick to them, and I'm really not trying to be a jerk. I'm just asking for a couple of tox screens we did during autopsies over the last few months so we can get it squared away with the insurance companies. Every one of the records I'm asking for is from a person who isn't with us anymore, and it's only a tox screen. What can I do with that? I'm not looking to get you into trouble, I just need a little help. Please."

There was a long pause and he could hear her considering. He actually felt kind of bad for her. One of the things he'd learned from Lopez, of all people, who turned out to be pretty good with computers, was that the weakest point in any secure network was the people, and that most hackers didn't break into the system, they talked someone into giving them access.

Hopefully, he'd be able to use these records for leverage and they'd never see the light of day, and this lady wouldn't have any issue with it after this call.

"If I do this and it comes back on me, I am giving them your name."

"Do that. No problem. It's Mark Jensen from Doctor Henley's office. The number and address are what you have on file. You can put that in your notes and throw me under the bus if anyone asks."

She let out a short breath.

"Fine. Give me the case numbers you need and the collection dates."

He picked up his pad and started reading off the reports that Henley had billed to the insurance company. There was a short silence, punctuated by more keystrokes.

"Okay, I see all those," she said, sounding maybe a little bit more comfortable when she saw they were for exactly what Taylor said they were.

"Great. Just send those through this one time. All of our other information should stay the same, since IT should have us back up and running in a couple of days."

"Fine. If the doctor has any questions, he can call us directly," she said.

"I'll tell him," Taylor said. "And thank you. You just saved me from a bad afternoon."

She made a disgruntled noise and disconnected.

He sat and waited, hoping she didn't change her mind. She didn't. A minute later, an email from the diagnostics company appeared in his inbox.

He opened it and saw six PDF icons waiting at the bottom of the message, each labeled with a case number.

He clicked the first one and watched it load. The lab used a standard format: header with patient initials, clinic name, ordering provider, dates, then a table of analytes with reference ranges and results. At the top, the bold line: Cause of death: traumatic injury. Toxicology: supplemental.

He went straight to the table.

Lead. Arsenic. Cadmium. Chromium. A few organic compounds he recognized from the drum placards in the mine. Each line had a column for reference range and a column for patient result.

In the Bradley case, three of the metals sat well above the lab's flagged limits, although according to the report, not enough to kill anyone right away, but enough to cause underlying health problems.

Problems that weren't a part of Bradley's cause of death, so no one thought twice about them.

Well, no one but the conspirators, who, if they saw this, would know exactly what it meant. This was a smoking gun for what they were doing. All these people with heightened levels of contaminants that could be found in the material Mountain Vista was recycling would at least lead to investigations and questions.

Investigations and questions Mountain Vista could not let happen.

It wasn't a bad plan on Henley's part. As leverage goes, this was pretty good, although odds were, if he actually threatened them with it, they would kill him rather than negotiate.

Now they make good leverage for Taylor to get Henley to flip on his partners.

Chapter 11

Taylor drove straight to the clinic and parked in the small lot in the back. He grabbed the folder with the toxicology reports and billing statements and headed for the entrance.

The receptionist looked up as he came through the door.

"Sir, do you have an appointment?" she said, standing as he started to walk past her, headed for the door to the inner office.

"No," he said, and kept walking past her, pushing the door open and turning down the hallway before she could say anything else.

The clinic was small enough that finding Henley's office wasn't hard. The second door on the left helpfully had his nameplate on the wall. Taylor pushed it open without knocking.

Henley was behind his desk, reading something on his computer. He looked up when Taylor came through the door, startled, his face going pale.

"Mister Taylor. What are you ...?"

Taylor stepped inside and closed the door behind him. He reached back and turned the lock.

"We need to talk."

"I told you everything I can. The sheriff ..."

"Shut ... up."

Taylor dropped the folder on the desk, its papers spilling out across the surface. Billing statements, test orders, and the lab reports with columns of numbers and reference ranges.

Henley stared at them. His mouth opened, then closed.

"You know what those are," Taylor said.

Henley's hand moved toward the papers, then stopped. He pulled it back and set it in his lap.

"I don't know what you think ..."

"Justin Bradley, Thomas Evans, Sarah Miller, Peter Olsen, Ryan Hall, Roy Breyer." Taylor pointed at the reports. "You ordered comprehensive toxicology screens on every single one of them, and you found something. Lead, arsenic, cadmium, chromium, each body came back with elevated levels of those metals and a bunch more shit. Not stuff six random people in a small town would have in them, but the exact kind of thing you'd find where there was a runoff of industrial waste."

Henley said nothing. His face had gone from pale to gray.

"You ruled them accidental deaths anyway, signed off on autopsy reports that didn't mention any of this, and let their families bury them without knowing what really happened to them. Without knowing they were murdered."

"I didn't ..."

"Yes! You! Did!" Taylor leaned forward, his hands flat on the desk. "You falsified official documents, covered up evidence, and helped Mountain Vista Industries hide what they were doing."

Henley's breath came faster as he looked at the door, then back at Taylor.

"You don't understand."

"Then explain it."

"I can't."

"You're going to," Taylor spat. He pulled out his phone and set it on the desk between them. "Right now, or I walk out of here and send every one of these reports to the FBI, to the EPA, to the Minnesota Attorney General's office, and the Minnesota Medical board! When they come asking questions, I'll make sure they know you were the one who signed the falsified death certificates."

Henley's hands trembled, and he clasped them together to make them stop.

"They'll kill me."

"What do you think will happen if I make those calls? Do you trust your partners enough to get rid of the evidence before everything falls apart ... starting with you? Tell me what happened. *It's your only choice.*"

Henley closed his eyes, and when he opened them again, some of the fear had been replaced by exhaustion.

"Bradley was the first. He came to me nine months ago complaining about headaches, nausea, joint pain, and I ran blood work and saw the elevated metals. I asked him about exposure, and he told me about how his cattle were getting sick."

"What did you do?"

"I reported it to the state health department, just like I was supposed to." Henley's voice was flat now, like he was reading from a script he'd practiced. "Three days later, Bradley's truck went off the road, and Sheriff Brody ruled it an accident. Wade Hutchins came to see me that same afternoon."

Taylor waited.

"He explained the situation. Mountain Vista had contracts worth hundreds of millions of dollars, jobs for the whole town, tax revenue for the county, and if word got out about contamination, even if it turned out to be nothing, the contracts would be canceled. The plant would close and the town would die."

"So you agreed to cover it up."

"I agreed to wait until they could investigate properly. Hutchins said they were bringing in their own environmental consultants, that they'd handle it internally and fix whatever was wrong." Henley looked down at his hands. "He offered me money, a retainer for consulting work, twenty thousand a year, and all I had to do was not make waves until they sorted it out. You don't understand how hard it is to maintain a practice in a small town like this. We were struggling to stay open, and if I shut my doors, the nearest doctor would be almost an hour away."

"So you took the money."

"Yes."

"And that's when they told you to start falsifying autopsy results."

"Yes. Every time someone died, Brody would call me and tell me what to write in the report while Hutchins would remind me that I'd already taken the money and could lose my license if people found out. And Brody, he talked about how my wife was at home while I was at work, all by herself, and how crime was getting harder to control with people out of work. I knew what he was saying. They had me trapped."

"Roy figured it out, didn't he? That's why you wouldn't release his body."

"Brody put a hold on releasing the body the morning after Roy died and said Hutchins needed time to clean up whatever Roy had found, that we couldn't let the family have the body until all the evidence was gone."

"What about the toxicology screens? Why did you keep ordering them if you were just going to bury the results?"

Henley looked at the reports on his desk.

"I thought if I had something on them, proof, documentation, something I could use if ..."

"If what?"

"If they ever came after me. I've been collecting evidence for months, everything I could document without them noticing."

Taylor had just been expecting the tox-screens, which were bad enough, although not exactly a smoking gun. If Henley had more though, he could shut this whole thing down.

"What kind of evidence?"

"These toxicology reports, pictures of the bodies and unedited autopsies, a few recordings of Brody and Hutchins telling me what to do."

"Where are they?"

Henley hesitated.

"You're already in this," Taylor said. "Everyone is going down, one way or another, so the only way out is through me. Where's the evidence?"

"At my house, in the gun safe in my bedroom. There's a binder with all the documents and a thumb drive with the audio recordings."

Taylor picked up his phone and the folder.

"Get up. We're leaving."

"What? Where ..."

"To your house. We're getting that binder and thumb drive, and then you're going somewhere safe until the FBI can take you into custody."

"I can't just leave. I ..."

"You're done here." Taylor opened the door. "I have enough on you with these to put you in jail for a long time. The feds are on their way, one way or another. You can wait until they arrest you, or maybe until your partners decide the walls are closing in and you're a weak link and *take care of you*, or you can cooperate. Your choice."

Henley stood up slowly and looked around his office like he was looking for a way out. But there wasn't one. Then he grabbed his coat from the hook on the wall and followed Taylor into the hallway.

The receptionist looked up as they passed.

"Doctor Henley, your two o'clock ..."

"Cancel my appointments for the rest of the day," Henley said without stopping.

They went out the back exit into the small parking lot behind the clinic. Taylor's rental sat alone near the far end, across the street, a dark blue sedan was parked along the curb. The driver was slouched in his seat with a coffee cup in his hand and two more empties on the dashboard.

Taylor had seen him before, one of the men who'd been hanging around since he arrived in town, not the three from the parking lot, but cut from the same cloth. Late thirties, thick build, trying too hard to look casual.

The man's head turned as they came out, his eyes going to Henley, then to Taylor, then back to Henley. For a second, he looked confused, and then his expression changed. Taylor's hand went to the small of his back, to pull his gun, but the guy started the car and took off, a cell phone already going up to his ear.

Taylor pushed Henley into the rental and pulled out of the parking lot in a hurry. They knew Henley was the weak link and with Taylor poking around, they'd left someone to keep an eye on his place.

"What's happening?" Henley asked.

"They've had someone watching you, probably ever since I got here."

"Oh God. We can't go to my house. They'll ..."

"Which is why we need to get there first."

Taylor pressed down on the accelerator. By now, Brody and whoever else Hutchins had on standby would be moving.

There was a good chance they were already behind.

Taylor drove past Henley's street and parked the rental three blocks over, tucked behind a delivery van that looked like it hadn't moved in a while. He killed the engine and sat for a moment, watching the rearview mirror for headlights that didn't come.

"Why are we stopping here?" Henley's voice had gone thin and reedy.

"Because if they're already at your house, pulling up in front would be stupid." Taylor opened his door and got out. "We walk from here."

Henley fumbled with his seatbelt and followed, stumbling a little as he got out of the car, letting out a little yelp as he fell to the ground, smacking his hands into the pavement to stop his fall.

Taylor grimaced. He led them through a narrow gap between two houses, cutting across a backyard, hoping to himself that there wasn't a dog.

They came out on Henley's street four houses down from his place. The neighborhood was older, the kind where trees had grown tall enough to cast deep shadows across the yards, and the houses sat far enough apart that people could pretend they didn't know what their neighbors were doing. Henley's house was a single-story ranch with faded blue siding and a detached garage.

They stopped at the edge of the property next door and checked the street. There weren't any cars that Henley didn't recognize, no movement in the windows, but the front door was open about six inches, which screamed setup.

"Is that how you left it this morning?"

"No. I locked it. I always lock it."

Taylor pulled his Glock from the holster at his back and kept it low against his thigh. "Stay behind me. If I tell you to run, you run, and you don't stop until you're somewhere public with people around."

"What about Julia?"

"If she's in there, we'll get her out. If she's not, standing out here talking about it won't help."

Taylor started forward, using the line of parked cars along the curb for cover.

They crossed the lawn in silence, Taylor's eyes on the door and the windows on either side. When they reached the small concrete porch, he could see the damage to the doorframe. The latch plate had been bent back, and the screws pulled partially out of the wood. Someone had forced it, and they hadn't cared about being subtle.

He pushed the door open with his foot and stepped inside, sweeping his weapon left to right across the entry hallway. The house was dim, curtains drawn against the afternoon sun, with only thin lines of daylight filtering through the windows. Furniture had been shoved away from the walls, drawers pulled out and dumped on the floor, cushions thrown off the couch in the living room to his right.

Henley came in behind him and stopped, staring at the wreckage of his living room. "Oh God. Julia ..."

"Quiet," Taylor said.

The kitchen was to the left, and through the doorway, Taylor could see more chaos, broken dishes scattered across the part of the floor he could see. A hallway led back toward what had to be bedrooms, and a door on the right stood open wider than the others, showing the edges of a desk and filing cabinet.

Two men stepped into view at the same time, one from the hallway and one from the kitchen doorway. The one from the hallway was the same man from the parking lot fight, the one whose nose Taylor had broken. White tape held it in place now, and his eyes had the predatory look of someone who'd been waiting for a chance to return the favor.

The other was older, maybe forty, with a shaved head and the thick build of someone who'd spent years doing manual labor. Both had pistols, and both had them pointed at Taylor and Henley.

"Hands up," the one with the broken nose said. "Nice and slow."

Taylor raised his left hand, keeping the Glock in his right but pointed at the floor. Beside him, Henley's hands shot up so fast he almost hit himself in the face.

"Gun on the floor," the older man said. "Two fingers, set it down easy."

Taylor crouched and placed the Glock on the floor, using his thumb and index finger like they'd asked. He stayed low for an extra second, taking in the scene and giving himself an extra moment to work the problem before straightening and raising his right hand to match his left.

"Back up. Both of you. Against the wall."

They shuffled backward until Taylor's shoulders hit the wall beside the front door. The two men came forward, keeping their weapons trained on them. Broken Nose moved to Taylor while the older man covered them both. He kicked Taylor's Glock across the room into the living area, then patted Taylor down, finding the backup pistol in Taylor's ankle holster, tossing it after the first one.

"Clear."

The older man shifted his aim fully onto Henley. "Doc, we need to talk."

Henley's hands trembled where he held them up beside his head. "I don't … I don't know what you want."

"Sure you do. Wade Hutchins wants your insurance policy, the recordings, and all of the documents you've been squirreling away. We know you've got them here somewhere."

"I don't …"

"Your wife told us about the safe." The older man let that sit for a moment, watching Henley's face crumple. "She's with Mister Hutchins now. Real nice lady, very cooperative once she understood the situation. If you want to see her again, you're going to open that safe and give us what's inside."

Henley turned to look at Taylor, and the expression on his face was pure hatred. "You did this. You came here and you pushed, and now they have Julia, and it's your fault."

"Doc …"

"No!" Henley's voice cracked, going high and desperate. "I was handling it. I was keeping everything quiet and safe, and then you showed up asking questions and tearing everything apart, and now Julia's gone, and it's all because of you!"

The older man gestured toward the open door on the right with his pistol. "Let's go, Doc. Nice and slow, and your friend stays right where he is."

Henley moved toward the doorway, his hands still up, his whole body shaking. Broken Nose kept his weapon on Taylor while the older man followed Henley into the den. From where Taylor stood, he could see part of the room through the open door: a desk, a filing cabinet, and the edge of a gun safe mounted against the far wall.

"Open it," the older man said from inside the den. "And if you're thinking about trying something clever, remember we've got your wife. You give us what we need, and she'll come home safe and sound. You don't and she disappears; you'll follow about ten seconds later."

Henley dropped to his knees in front of the safe, his hands fumbling with the combination dial. Both men had shifted their attention to Henley now, focused on what they'd come for.

It was an amateur move. Broken Nose should have stayed focused on Taylor and let his partner handle Henley, but guys like this, they were more used to roughing people up than controlling threats.

Broken Nose still had his pistol pointed in Taylor's general direction, but his eyes kept flicking toward the den, watching his partner. The older man had moved deeper into the room, positioning himself where he could see both Henley and the safe's interior. Neither of them was looking directly at Taylor anymore.

Taylor's hands were still raised beside his head, but his weight had shifted onto the balls of his feet. Broken Nose had gotten too close to him, only a step or two away. The man's pistol was pointed at Taylor's chest, but his finger was alongside the trigger guard instead of on the trigger itself, a good habit for guys who trained on the range, but not something a guy with combat experience would do. It added a fraction of a second to the reaction time, and in combat, that could be the difference between life and death.

"There," Henley said from inside the den. "It's open."

Broken Nose turned even more, leaning to see inside the den at what the older guy, who'd stepped toward the gun safe and out of the line of sight, was doing. His gun moved with him when he did, pointing at the wall next to Taylor by a fraction.

Taylor dropped his hands and lunged forward, closing the distance to Broken Nose fast. His right hand clamped down on the man's wrist, pulling the pistol flat against his side while his left hand drove up into the man's throat. Broken Nose made a choking sound and pulled the trigger. The pistol fired with a sharp crack, the bullet punching through the den wall.

Taylor twisted hard, snapping the man's wrist with an audible pop, then his trigger finger.

The older man shouted something when his partner fired into the room and came back into view, probably trying to figure out why his partner had shot in his direction, although his weapon was still pointed in toward Henley.

Taylor ripped the pistol from Broken Nose's ruined hand, his fingers closing around the grip as he shoved the man backward, causing him to trip over his feet and flail as he fell backward. Taylor ignored him for the moment and pivoted toward the den doorway.

The older man, realizing what was happening, started to turn his weapon toward the threat. Taylor didn't hesitate, he fired twice. The first round caught the man high in the chest and the second a few fingers lower. He went down, making a sucking sound and clutching at his chest.

Broken Nose had rolled over and started to scramble toward Taylor's gun, which had been kicked across the room. Taylor pointed down and fired once, punching a bullet through the back of the man's head and into the hardwood floor.

The silence afterward was broken only by Henley's high, panicked breathing from inside the den.

Taylor checked the older man, ignoring Broken Nose, who wouldn't be moving again. He wasn't quite dead yet and looked up into Taylor's eyes with the expression of a man who was surprised where his choices had taken him.

And then he gave a last, rattled exhale, his eyes glazing over.

Taylor retrieved his Glock and backup pistol from where they'd been kicked, holstering both, before going into the den where Henley was still on his knees in front of the open safe, looking equal parts shocked and sick.

"You killed them," Henley said. "You killed them, and now ... now Julia's dead. That was the only way to get her back, and you just ..."

"That was never going to get her back."

"You don't know that!"

"I absolutely know that. Once you handed over the files, they were going to kill you and me and then call Hutchins and confirm they had the evidence. Hutchins would have Julia killed to tie up that loose end. That's how this works, Doc. You don't leave witnesses when you're covering up multiple murders."

"But they said ..."

"They lied," Taylor said, crouching beside the safe and looking inside.

A thick binder stuffed with papers sat on the top shelf, next to a thumb drive in a plastic case and several bundles of cash wrapped in rubber bands. He pulled out the binder and thumb drive and tucked them under his arm.

"This is what they wanted. Your insurance policy."

Henley's hands were still shaking. "Then Julia's already dead. If what you're saying is true, then they've already ..."

"No. She's alive because she's leverage. They took her to make sure you'd cooperate, and they won't kill her until they're certain the evidence is gone." Taylor stood and offered his hand. "He must have had your office bugged. It's the only explanation for why they'd go for your insurance policy now. I'm sure as hell that they wouldn't have let you keep that kind of incriminating evidence around if they'd known about it. But he doesn't know how long it will take us to get here, if they'd have to beat you to get the safe open, or what I was going to do. So we have a window of opportunity. Eventually, these guys aren't going to check in, and Hutchins will start wondering. He'll call and won't get an answer. You're still a problem, though, so he can't just kill Julia. He'll probably send other guys here to find out what happened to these two. Then ... who knows. They hold on to her in case they find you, or they start scrubbing everything down and get rid of any loose ends they can, which would include her. Either way, we don't have time to stand here and talk. The clock is ticking."

Henley took the hand that Taylor held out and let him pull him to his feet. His face had gone gray and waxy, the look of a man who'd run out of options and knew it.

"What do we do?"

"I'm going to put you somewhere safe, and then I'm going to get your wife back."

Chapter 12

Taylor got Henley back in the car and pulled back onto the state road, headed northeast toward the hills. The binder and thumb drive were in Henley's lap, wrapped in a plastic grocery bag Taylor had found in the trunk, although the doctor barely seemed to notice them.

Now that the adrenaline of the moment was fading, Henley was starting to feel how close that situation was. Taylor didn't blame him. Your first time that close to death could mess anyone up.

"Where are we going?" Henley finally asked as they left the town, the hills getting closer.

"No offense, Doc, but you're a liability in a firefight. I need a place to stash you so I can get your wife out safely without having to worry about keeping you alive, too, and I'm going to need you to stay alive so you can testify. A friend of Roy's lives up in the hills, off the grid. Nobody's going to look for you there, and if they do, they'll have a hell of a time getting close without him knowing about it."

"But then you'll get Julia back, right?"

"I told you I would, and I will. Besides, she's now a direct witness to their crimes, so it makes the case even stronger."

"But how? You can't just walk into Mountain Vista and demand her back. They'll just kill her. You don't know Hutchins. He's ruthless."

"Trust me, I've known a lot of guys much worse than Wade Hutchins," Taylor said, thinking back to some of the gangsters, tribal warlords, and jihadists he'd faced since getting out of the service.

Henley didn't seem to believe him; he just stared out the windshield, not saying anything else. They pulled off the state road and onto the dirt track that led up into the hills, past the closed mine, now blown shut. He'd been here less than twenty-four hours earlier, but it felt like a year ago.

It was late afternoon when Morrison's cabin came into view. Smoke rose from the chimney, and Taylor could see Morrison's truck parked beside the cabin, in exactly the same spot it had been in the day before. He pulled the rental in next to it and killed the engine.

Morrison appeared on the porch before they got out, the rifle in his hands as usual. He looked at Taylor, then at Henley, and his expression went from cautious to hostile.

"So he was in on it," Morrison said, glaring at the doctor.

"He was," Taylor said.

To his surprise, Morrison came down off the porch and got an inch from Henley's face.

"You ought to burn for what you did. Roy was a good man."

"I didn't mean ..." Henley said, looking to Taylor, scared of how intently Morrison was looking at him.

"You're why the land around here is getting poisoned, forcing us out of our homes."

"I didn't do anything. They threatened me. Made me sign the death certificates."

"He's a coward, that's true," Taylor said. "And that actually works in our favor. It seems the good doctor here was so scared his partners might turn on him that he made an insurance policy detailing everything they were doing. And since they just tried to kill him, he's agreed to testify against them, which means that we now actually have a case to go after them."

Morrison made an unimpressed grunting noise and spat in the dirt at his feet, but at least he backed away from Henley.

"What do you want from me?" he asked, looking to Taylor.

"Some more help. They grabbed his wife, and she's being held at the Mountain Vista facility by Hutchins and his goons. Doc here might be a scumbag, but his wife didn't do anything to deserve this. I need to go get her, but I can't do it with him weighing me down. I need to stash him to keep him alive long enough to make sure Wade Hutchins spends the rest of his life in a federal prison," Taylor said, and held up the plastic bag. "This is his insurance policy. Copies of the falsified autopsy, toxicology reports showing heavy metal contamination in the victims, and audio recordings of Brody and Hutchins making threats. These, along with his testimony, are enough to put them away."

Morrison looked back to Henley, and Taylor waited as he made up his mind. The man loved these hills, clearly, and he was pissed at what Hutchins was doing to them, and Henley was part of that. Taylor hoped that his wanting to get revenge on Hutchins was enough for him to let Henley off the hook.

Finally, he looked at Taylor and jerked his head toward the cabin. "Get inside. Both of you."

Morrison gestured for them toward a rough wooden table while he leaned the rifle against the wall within easy reach. Taylor set the plastic bag on the table.

"I already have some people at the FBI in the know about what's happening here, and this is enough to bring them down here, so I just need you to keep him safe until they get here. I don't know how things will go with Hutchins, but I'll give my contact your number and directions to get here. They'll come and take him off your hands, so one way or another, Hutchins is going down. I'll leave this stuff with you, too, just in case."

Morrison stood and picked up the binder.

"I'll put this somewhere safe. You," he said, pointing at Henley. "Sit there and don't move."

Henley sat down and looked shell-shocked.

Morrison disappeared into a back room, taking the binder and thumb drive with him. Taylor heard drawers opening, something heavy being moved across the floor.

"Don't run. Hutchins will be looking for you, and you know what they'll do if they find you. So stay put."

Henley just nodded, looking at his hands.

"How long before the Feds show up?" Morrison said, coming back into the room.

"Depends on how fast my partner can move. They'll probably get local agents rolling out of Minneapolis, but that will still take four or five hours. They'll be here tonight, though."

"And you're going after Hutchins now."

"That's right."

"Alone."

"No time for anything else. It won't be long until they realize Henley's flown the coop, and they decide they need to get rid of his wife. I need to get to her before then."

Henley let out a whimper.

Morrison grunted again and then said, "I'll keep the doctor safe."

"Thanks," Taylor said, shaking his hand and heading for the door.

He walked far enough from the cabin that Morrison and Henley wouldn't overhear, pulled out his phone and dialed Whitaker's number. She answered on the second ring.

"Where are you?"

"Morrison's cabin. I have the doctor; he's agreed to testify, and he has a lot of hard evidence, including audio recordings. It's solid and prosecutable, enough to bury Hutchins and Brody both."

"Music to my ears," she said. "I'll coordinate with the Bureau's Minneapolis field office, get warrants issued for Mountain Vista, Hutchins, Brody, and anyone else involved. We can have federal agents on the ground tonight."

"Good. I have Henley stashed with Morrison. I'll text you his address."

"Where are you going to be?"

"They grabbed Henley's wife to force him to hand over the evidence. I dealt with those guys, but they're holding her at the Mountain Vista plant. I'm going to go get her before they can do anything stupid."

Silence on the other end of the line, and Taylor could picture Whitaker's expression, the way her mouth would set when she knew he was about to do something she couldn't stop.

"John ..."

"They'll kill her to tie up the loose end, and there isn't time for you to do anything about it. The locals are corrupt, so I don't even know where you'd get a team to rescue her. State troopers, maybe, but they'll be an hour out, and it'll just be some guys in patrol cars. Hutchins' men aren't pros, but there are a bunch of them, and they're armed. If they get backed into a corner, things could go bad."

"Which is an argument for you not going in by yourself. This isn't the smart play."

"It's the only play, and I've dealt with worse odds. You know it. I can handle them. Morrison will keep Henley and the evidence safe. Your agents can pick them both up from Morrison when they arrive. But I'm not sitting here waiting for permission while Julia runs out of time."

"They won't do anything for a few hours, probably. Wait two hours. Give me two hours to get someone to back you up."

Taylor looked down the mountain toward where the lights of Glacier Falls would be visible once full dark settled in. He thought about Julia Henley sitting in some room, terrified and alone, while men with guns decided whether she lived or died.

"I'm not going to take that chance."

"Taylor ..."

"This isn't a discussion, I'm going. Tell your agents to expect Morrison and Henley at the cabin."

He ended the call and turned the phone to silent before sliding it back into his pocket. She would keep trying to talk him into waiting, both because she didn't want him hurt and because it was procedure. Better to just do what he had to do and ask for forgiveness later.

Taylor walked to the rental and started the engine. Through the cabin window, he could see Henley sitting at the table with his head in his hands, and Morrison standing in the doorway with his rifle. Neither of them moved as Taylor backed the car around.

The sun was starting to go down as he got back on the state road and headed for town.

When he reached the turn off for the plant, Taylor turned the headlights off for the last stretch, letting the pale light wash from the plant guide him in, easing the rental onto the shoulder and rolling to a stop where the gravel access road curved toward the main gate.

He killed the engine and listened for a few seconds, checking if someone had noticed him or if there were any other vehicles coming. When it seemed clear, he popped the trunk and stepped out into the cold. He'd made a stop at the hardware store on the edge of town on his way in, and now pulled the results of that trip out of the trunk. Inside a plastic bag were wire cutters, a small flashlight with a covered lens, a bunch of small washcloths, and two bundles of extra-long plastic zip ties. The ties were cheap, but they'd do the job.

Trunk shut, he crossed the ditch and slipped into the trees, moving parallel to the access road, keeping the chain-link fence in sight ahead.

He stopped when he reached the line where the trees thinned and went to one knee behind a fallen log. From here, he could see the main gate and the front of the building. Floodlights mounted on tall poles washed the parking lot and the main building.

Five vehicles sat in the lot near the front doors. Day shift gone and what had to be a skeleton crew inside.

He counted the guards he could see.

One was at the corner near the tanks, rifle hooked on a sling. Another worked along the loading dock at the side of the building, near the trailers and roll-up door. A third and fourth were walking together on a loose circuit, cutting from the rear lot along the east wall, then arcing past the front of the building and around toward the tanks off to one side before vanishing behind the structure again.

They weren't in uniforms, but they all carried civilian-make rifles and wore the same cheap mail-order plate carriers, so probably the same amateurs he'd seen all along, and not some new group of professionals.

He watched two full loops of the moving pair, getting a sense for how long they spent on each side of the building. The dock man walked his route on a slow line from one end to the other, head turning in short arcs. He'd at least had some formal training, maybe a short stint in the service. The man by the tanks didn't move much at all. He mostly stared at his phone.

When the roving pair went around the far corner again, Taylor backed into the trees and moved left, following the outside of the fence until he saw the small maintenance shed near the northwest edge of the property.

The fence ran close to the shed here, only a narrow strip of gravel between chain-link and corrugated metal. The light from the yard poles fell short, leaving a wedge of shadow where brush had grown up under the fence.

He crouched at that point and pushed the brush aside with his forearm. The chain-link sagged a little under his touch. He put the jaws of the cutters around one of the bottom strands and squeezed, the wire parting with a faint crunch. He cut again, working in a rough rectangle the width of his shoulders, then pushed the loosened section up just enough to crawl through on his stomach.

The fence scraped his back but didn't snag. He came up on the inside and pushed the section back into place behind him. If someone got up close, they'd see it was cut, but from ten feet away, it'd look undisturbed.

He stayed low and moved along the shadow of the shed until it blended into the first row of filtration tanks.

The first guard stood twenty yards away on a strip of concrete beside the outermost tank. Sodium light from a pole over his head washed his features. Rifle on his shoulder, phone in his hand, boot on a short step as he scrolled with his thumb.

He studied the space between them. There was enough cover for a patient approach.

He moved in stages, body close to the steel when he crossed open ground. His boots found bare spots on the concrete, places where no grit waited to crunch, trying to move as quietly as he could. Every few steps, he stopped and watched, giving the guard time to turn by chance, and ready to rush him if he did. Taylor didn't need to worry, though. The guy's attention stayed locked to his phone.

At the last tank, he paused, about ten yards away. He studied the angles of the man's elbows and shoulders, then stepped out in a straight line when the guard shifted his weight and lifted his hand to scratch his cheek.

Two quick steps closed the space, coming in at an angle. His left arm looped around the man's neck, forearm pressed against the front of the throat, biceps against one side, his forearm pinning the other. His right hand caught the back of the guard's head and pulled it in against his chest.

The rifle swung as the man's body lurched, but Taylor pinned the sling line with his elbow and pulled backward, taking their combined weight onto his hips. The guard's hands shot up and clawed at the arm on his throat for a few seconds, then they lost strength.

The first rush of resistance lasted for about five heartbeats; after that, it turned into uncoordinated tapping at his sleeve. Taylor held the choke and counted to fifteen in his head, then eased the pressure and shifted his stance to lower the body to the concrete. The man sagged, eyes half-closed, chest moving in shallow draws of air.

Alive, although he probably wouldn't be out for long.

Taylor rolled him onto his stomach, pulled the man's wrists together behind his back, and zip-tied them in place. He then did the same thing with his legs, zip-tied at the ankles. His last step was to pull the man's jaws open, shove in a washcloth, and then pull a zip-tie across his open mouth and around the back of his head.

It was a tight fit, even with the longer ties, and the edges of the plastic were cutting into the corners of his mouth really badly. That would hurt like hell when he came to, but it would make it harder to scream for help when he woke up.

He popped the clips on the man's vest and checked his pockets. Wallet, folding knife, spare magazines for the rifle. On the vest, a small plastic badge on a retractable cord held an ID card with the Mountain Vista logo and the man's name. He tugged the cord loose from the vest and clipped it onto his own belt. The man's radio sat on his shoulder strap. Taylor unfastened it and slid it into a pocket of his jacket.

He eased the rifle off the sling and set it on the ground, barrel pointed away from both of them. He was half-tempted to take it with him, but if he started firing, there was a good chance someone might put a bullet in Julia just to silence her, so it was better to stay with the quiet approach.

Which meant leaving his hands free to subdue the other guards he needed to deal with.

He hooked his hands under the guard's coat and dragged him into the shadow of a concrete pump housing, where pipes and a short stairwell pushed out from the side of a tank. To someone looking from the main yard, the man would be nothing more than another shape in the dark.

One down.

The loading dock sat ahead to his right, a metal platform and roll-up doors raised above a rectangle of asphalt. A semi-trailer sat at one bay, tractor gone, the back doors closed. Floodlights pointed down over the dock area, bright enough that shadows under the trailer turned into a single dark block.

The second guard walked a long line along the edge of the dock, rifle held with both hands at a low angle, muzzle pointed a few feet ahead of him. He moved with slow steps, eyes and head in motion, scanning the lot and then the tanks. He paused now and then to look along the tree line or up toward the riverside of the plant.

Taylor slid behind the front of the semi-trailer, keeping the big rectangle of white metal between himself and the dock lights.

He watched the guard pace.

From the corner of the dock to the far end, then back along the trailer, then a pause while he looked up toward the road. No conversation, no phone.

The man walked past the nose of the trailer and, as he moved along the side of the trailer again, Taylor stepped out from under the front overhang, the trailer blocking them from the view of the main lot.

The guard's attention stayed out toward the yard, and there was no reason for him to think someone'd come from the blind side of a parked trailer.

At three feet, Taylor reached forward with his left hand and caught a fistful of the man's jacket at the shoulder and yanked hard, pulling the man back and down, off balance, while his right hand came up with the pistol. He drove the hard back of the slide into the base of the guard's skull where it met the neck.

The guard sagged as the weapon made contact, his knees folding. Taylor rode him down, one hand on the jacket, the other already moving the pistol away from the man's body. The rifle clattered against the dock edge but stayed in its sling.

The man lay on his side, limbs slack, chest still moving. Taylor grabbed the front of his vest and dragged him under the trailer, into the deep strip of shadow along the centerline where he repeated the binding that he'd done on the first man, except with an extra tie through this one's belt and then around the crossbar under the trailer.

It wouldn't hold forever, not with the weight being put on it, but it would make it harder for the guy to roll out from under the trailer when he woke up.

Still, the roving pair would notice this guy missing when they came past on their route. They didn't pass the tank guy, but they did pass by this spot. He needed to deal with them before he went inside.

He circled the rear of the trailer and moved along the wall of the building toward the front. The access doors at the dock were all roll-ups and there was a heavy metal man door with a crash bar inside. No access from there. He passed a small side entrance with a card reader and keypad, and kept going until he reached the front corner of the administration wing.

Here, the plant changed from industrial steel to glass and brick. Windows lined the second floor, blinds drawn behind them. A wide set of glass doors formed the main entrance, under a flat awning with the Mountain Vista logo on it.

Taylor stayed at the corner where brick met steel, shoulder against the wall, face turned toward the parking lot. The two roving guards came into view from the far side, cutting along the east wall and heading toward the front.

They walked side by side, rifles slung this time, a coffee cup in the hand of one, a cigarette in the other's fingers, their voices making it unlikely they'd hear anything else but each other.

They reached the front row of parking spaces and turned toward the entrance, angling along the glass doors. Their route took them parallel to the wall where Taylor waited, close enough for him to touch them if he stepped out at the right moment.

He put his hand on the butt of the Glock and waited as they drew near. The man with the cigarette was talking and the one with the coffee laughed at something he said. When they were almost past his corner, Taylor moved.

He stepped out behind the one with the coffee and brought the pistol up in a short arc, bringing it down on the soft spot behind the ear. The man's knees went out from under him, and he collapsed, the coffee cup flying from his hand.

The second guard turned in surprise, gawking at the sudden violence, just as Taylor caught a handful of his jacket and yanked him forward. The concrete wall beside the doors was a foot away, and Taylor propelled the man's head right into it with all of his weight behind the push. Skull hit brick, and the guard's hands flailed for a second before dropping.

Taylor hooked the first man by his collar and dragged him along the front of the building, through the line of shrubs, tying him up and rolling him into the plants. He then got the second guy, who was a little too limp and might be more seriously injured, and followed suit.

His pockets had the same things as the other guards: radio, lose change, and a key card. He also had a set of keys on him. A few office keys and a vehicle key. Taylor pocketed them, just in case they opened one of the doors inside.

If someone didn't want brain damage, they probably shouldn't take jobs as enforcers for a corrupt businessman murdering locals in the name of money.

There was still no chatter on his stolen radio.

Taylor moved back to the main entrance where he'd seen a card reader next to the glass doors, a simple black rectangle with a red LED at the top. He pulled the ID card from his belt and passed it in front of the reader.

The light turned green, and the lock gave a soft click. He pulled one of the doors open just wide enough to slip through and then eased it shut behind him.

Inside, a security desk stood empty off to one side. He paused for a moment and listened. There were no footsteps and no voices close by.

Taking that as a good sign, he moved behind the desk. A plastic tray of visitor badges, a landline phone, a printer, but no logbook. A camera bubble in the ceiling pointed toward the doors, which wasn't great. If anyone was watching it, they'd have seen him strolling in.

He filed that away. If they hadn't raised an alarm by now, either no one was watching or the feed went to a recorder in a back room with no live eyes on it.

Office doors lined the right side of the hallway, each with a small plaque: Human Resources, Accounting, Logistics. He checked two at random, turning the knobs and cracking the doors for a peek inside. Both rooms sat empty, screens dark, chairs pushed under desks.

The double doors at the far end had small panes of wire-reinforced glass set at eye height. Beyond them, he saw the high ceiling and bright lights of the production floor he'd been shown that morning, with its rows of pipes and catwalks.

The guys waiting in Henley's house said Hutchins had Julia, and Taylor could only assume that meant in Hutchins' office, or nearby, which was here in the administrative wing. To be safe, he zip-tied the handles of the doors to the production floor together with three ties. Not impregnable, but it would slow anyone coming from that direction and coming in behind him. Going down the hallway, more doors lined both sides, each with brass nameplates: Operations Manager, Compliance, Legal.

At an intersection ahead, the hall broke left and right. Straight ahead, it ended at a blank wall with a painting of a river canyon. Turning left would lead toward another row of offices, but Hutchins had taken Taylor to his office that morning.

He'd turned right.

At the end of the corridor, a wider door waited, flanked by two tall indoor plants in square pots and a polished metal plaque beside the frame that read Executive Offices, W. Hutchins, CEO.

The lights were on inside, and he could see the shadow of a person against one wall visible through the window next to the door.

Chapter 13

Taylor pushed through the door with his Glock up and leveled.

Hutchins stood behind his desk, phone pressed to his ear. He froze mid-sentence, eyes tracking from Taylor's face to the pistol and back again.

"John," he said. "I didn't expect you to make it this far."

Taylor did not answer. He kept the Glock trained on the center of Hutchins's chest and moved three steps into the room, closing the door behind him and putting the desk between him and it, giving himself an angle on both the window and the hallway behind him.

The office was large, thirty feet by twenty. Glass shelves lined one wall, holding awards and framed photographs, and the windows had the blinds drawn, slats tilted to block the view from outside.

"Where's Julia Henley?"

Hutchins set the phone down with a soft click. He studied Taylor's face, like he was working out a puzzle.

"You took out my men?"

"Where is she?"

"All of them?"

Taylor said nothing, and Hutchins nodded slowly. "That's impressive. I thought we had enough men out there to slow you down, at least."

"Last time. Where's Julia Henley?"

"She's not here."

"Wrong answer."

"It's the truth." Hutchins lowered his hands an inch, testing. Taylor's aim did not shift, and Hutchins stopped moving. "She's alive. Safe, but not here."

"Then where?"

He didn't answer for a moment, clearly considering, before saying, "Sheriff Brody has her."

Taylor kept the pistol steady. His left hand moved to his jacket pocket and came out with a zip tie, tossing it onto the desk between them.

"Hands behind your back."

Hutchins looked at the tie, then back at Taylor, not moving to pick it up. "You're not thinking this through."

"One of us isn't."

"Brody has Milly Breyer, too."

Taylor went still.

Hutchins saw his reaction and pressed on. "Brody picked her up an hour ago. She's sharing a cell right now with Julia Henley."

"You're lying."

"We can call them, if you want."

Taylor wasn't dumb enough to take that offer.

Hutchins lowered his hands another inch. His voice stayed calm, reasonable. "You're smart, John, and you know how this works. Brody has both women. You kill me, you walk away, you call your friends at the FBI, those women disappear. Brody makes it look like you did it and pins a few things on you besides. Sure, you have friends and it won't stick, but by the time anyone sorts out the truth, Brody's long gone and those women are still dead."

"And what will you give me if I cooperate?"

Hutchins opened his mouth to answer, and then paused, a small smile escaping his lips. "Except you'd never consider it, not for a moment. I read about you, remember? Ever the Boy Scout with your FBI agent wife. Maybe we should invite her down to help with the investigation, clear your name. She can have a spot next to the other two."

Taylor adjusted his grip on the Glock, lifting it a little higher. "You should stop talking."

"I'm just making a point, John, that we hold all the ..."

Taylor stepped forward and brought the Glock down in a short, chopping arc, the butt of the grip catching Hutchins above the left ear with a sound like a mallet hitting a sandbag. Hutchins's eyes rolled white, and he dropped sideways, catching the arm of his chair on the way down, spinning it as he collapsed onto the carpet.

Taylor came around the desk and stood over him. Hutchins lay on his side, mouth open, breathing in shallow pulls; a red welt was already rising on his temple.

He grabbed a handful of Hutchins's suit jacket and rolled him onto his stomach. He pulled his wrists together behind his back and zip-tied them together, cinching the plastic before doing the ankles the same way. As with the guards, he shoved a washcloth into Hutchins's mouth and secured it with another tie looped around his head, the plastic biting into the corners of his lips.

Not so much to keep him from alerting anyone else, though. He just didn't want to hear the man blabber on anymore.

Hutchins weighed maybe one hundred seventy, heavy but doable. Taylor hooked his hands under the man's armpits and dragged him across the carpet, through the office door, and into the hallway.

Now it was about speed, not stealth.

He moved fast down the corridor, pulling Hutchins along the polished floor as fast as he could drag him, his pistol still in his hand, tucked under the businessman's armpit. Taylor passed the intersection and turned, heading toward the lobby and the main entrance.

He was twenty feet from the security desk when the first alarm went off.

Someone had found one of the guards.

He increased his pace as much as he could, pulling Hutchins through the lobby, past the empty desk, and hitting the front door with his shoulder. The glass swung wide, and cool air rushed in. The alarm was louder out here, a steady electronic wail bouncing off the concrete and steel. Off in the distance, men shouted from somewhere behind the building. They'd found their missing friends and sounded the alarms.

He was short on time.

The administrative parking lot was right in front of him with five vehicles in the front row. His rental, however, sat two hundred yards beyond the front gate, on the gravel shoulder where he'd left it.

He'd never make it there, but a white Chevy Tahoe with the Mountain Vista logo on the door sat fifteen feet from the entrance in one of the parking spots. Maybe one of the guys on patrol's vehicle. He pulled out the set of keys he'd taken off one of the roving guards. There was a car key with a Chevy logo on it.

Maybe he'd get lucky. If not, he could always hotwire it.

He dragged Hutchins across the pavement. The man's heels scraped against the concrete, his bound hands trailing behind him like dead weight. A door banged open on the east side of the building, followed by footsteps and someone yelling.

Taylor reached the Tahoe and tried the rear hatch. Unlocked. He grabbed Hutchins by the collar and belt, bent his knees, and heaved. The man went into the cargo area face-first, landing hard on the carpeted floor with a muffled grunt. He'd feel that when this was all over. Taylor slammed the hatch and moved around to the driver's side.

The door was unlocked.

Taylor dropped into the seat, put the borrowed key in the ignition, and turned it. Luck was with him, and the engine caught on the first try. He threw the transmission into drive and stomped on the accelerator.

He saw two guards come tearing around the corner of the building as he shot across the parking lot.

The first round hit the passenger door before the vehicle had moved ten feet; the bullet punched through the sheet metal with a flat crack and buried itself in the center console, spraying plastic fragments across his right arm. Taylor ducked low behind the wheel and kept his foot down on the accelerator.

The Tahoe surged forward. More shots came and muzzle flashes strobed against the dark. One round hit the rear quarter panel with a dull thunk, and another punched through the back window, blowing it out entirely, glass spraying across the cargo area and peppering Hutchins.

A third round flew past Taylor's head and shattered the rearview mirror.

He cut the wheel hard right, putting the engine block between himself and the shooters. The Tahoe fishtailed on the cold pavement, its rear end swinging wide. He corrected and aimed for the service gate fifty yards ahead. A rolling chain-link barrier on a motorized track, twelve feet high and closed.

But chain-link was just wire and aluminum posts, and the Tahoe weighed six thousand pounds.

Behind him, Hutchins slid across the cargo floor and thumped against the wheel well hard, letting out a moan. The guards were still firing, rounds hitting the tailgate in a rapid sequence. Cold air roared through the empty window frame.

He kept his foot on the accelerator. The speedometer climbed past forty. Forty-five.

The gate filled the windshield, and he braced his arms against the wheel, ducking his chin to his chest.

The SUV slammed into the gate.

The chain-link buckled at the center and tore away from the track on both sides, and the Tahoe lurched hard, the front-end dipping as something caught underneath. The gate wrapped around the hood and scraped across the roof with a shriek of tortured metal. Something caught the side mirror and ripped it off. The gate motor, bolted to a concrete pad, broke loose and tumbled under the chassis with a grinding crunch that shuddered through the frame.

It was hell on the Tahoe, but he was through.

The access road curved ahead, gravel and hard-packed dirt, trees pressing close on both sides. Taylor fought the wheel as the Tahoe bounced over ruts and washboard ridges. The steering pulled hard to the left now, and it was difficult to keep it under control. Something must have bent or been knocked loose in the front suspension. It was annoying, but not bad enough to stop him. He compensated and kept his speed up. Behind him, Hutchins groaned, but he was still out of it, maybe more so now with all the slamming around he'd taken back there.

In the remaining side mirror, the facility shrank with every passing second, the floodlights, flashing red strobes, and running figures growing smaller.

He drove another four miles, fighting the pull in the steering the whole way, but he kept the car moving.

He was more than halfway to town when his phone buzzed in his jacket pocket. He pulled it out with his right hand, keeping his left on the wheel, the steering pulling hard, fighting him.

He answered.

"John Taylor," Sheriff Brody said. "I hear you've been busy."

Taylor said nothing.

"Someone from the plant called me five minutes ago. Told me you walked out of there with Wade Hutchins. Is that true?"

"It's true."

"Where are you now?"

"Driving."

"Where to?"

Taylor didn't answer.

"You've got a problem, Taylor. I've got something you want, and you've got something I want. That's the definition of a deal waiting to happen."

Taylor drove another one hundred yards before he spoke again. "What do you want?"

"You bring me Wade, the Doc, and whatever insurance policy he was hiding, and I let Julia and Milly walk. Simple trade."

"And if I don't?"

"Then their deaths are on your head."

Taylor drove in silence.

"So what's it going to be, Taylor?"

"Where?"

"My office in one hour."

"I'll be there."

"Smart man. Now, I know your type. You're probably trying to think of a way to get out of this, something creative. Don't. I've got deputies all over town, and they're watching for you. You come in clean, or you don't come in at all."

The line went dead.

Taylor set the phone on the center console. The damaged Tahoe rattled and pulled left, but it held together.

He drove another six miles, following the access road until it joined the county highway. The clock on the dash showed 9:47 p.m. He had fifty-three minutes until Brody's deadline.

The highway curved ahead, cutting through a stretch of dense pines where darkness walled in both sides, unbroken by streetlights or houses. Taylor slowed and checked the shoulder ahead.

A sheriff's cruiser sat thirty feet off the pavement, tucked into a gravel turnout between two large pines. The car faced the highway, headlights off, but the engine running, making it easier to pick out.

Taylor had left the headlights off and it was dark, so it was unlikely the guy had seen him yet.

He slowed and pulled off to the side of the road, well ahead of the turnout, and down a few feet of a logging trail barely visible between the trees.

Behind him, Hutchins groaned again, louder this time. Taylor ignored him. He grabbed his weapon from the passenger seat, and checked the magazine. Seventeen rounds. Enough.

Climbing out, he went around to the back and popped the latch. With two more zip ties, he attached Hutchins to the frame of one of the seats by his hands and feet. It wasn't impossible to get out of, but it would be hard, especially for someone soft like Hutchins. That done, he moved back toward the highway on foot, staying inside the tree line.

Four minutes later, he reached a position twenty yards behind the cruiser. The car hadn't moved and its engine was still idling. Through the rear window, he could see the silhouette of a single deputy in the driver's seat. The man's head turned left, watching the highway, then right, then back down to his phone where it stayed for several minutes.

No wonder he'd been able to pull off without being seen so easily. This guy wasn't paying attention at all.

Taylor circled, moving through the trees until he came up on the passenger side of the cruiser. He stayed low, using the car's bulk for cover, and approached the front quarter panel. The deputy's window was closed.

Taylor moved to the passenger door in two quick steps, pulled it open, and leveled the Glock at the deputy's head.

"Don't move."

The deputy froze. His right hand had moved down to his sidearm in a natural reaction before stopping just above it as his brain caught up. Not that he could have gotten to it quickly. The holster was still clipped closed, giving him one more step he'd need to take to get it free.

He was older than Taylor, maybe forty, with gray at his temples and the thick build of someone who didn't do PT much.

Or ever.

"Both hands on the wheel," Taylor said.

The deputy obeyed. His hands moved slowly, deliberately, until they rested at ten and two.

"You alone?"

The guy glared at him and said, "Yeah."

"Good. Using your left hand, unclip your radio and drop it on the seat."

The deputy's left hand moved to his shoulder, fumbling with the radio clip. It came free and fell onto the passenger seat.

"Now the gun. Two fingers. Slow."

The deputy's right hand moved to his holster, thumb releasing the retention strap before he pulled it free with his thumb and forefinger, holding it like it might explode, and set it on the seat next to the radio.

"Keys."

"They're in the ignition."

No shit, Taylor thought.

"Turn off the vehicle and pull them out, then drop them on the seat," he said, explaining.

The deputy complied, and the keys landed on the seat.

"Out of the car. Slow."

The deputy opened his door and climbed out, hands raised.

"Walk around the front of the car and come here." The guy obeyed and Taylor stood, following him around, keeping his fire line straight.

"Turn around and put your hands behind your back."

The deputy turned and Taylor pulled a zip tie from his jacket pocket and secured the deputy's wrists, cinching the plastic.

"Around to the passenger door," Taylor said.

When the guy got there, Taylor edged around him, keeping his weapon from getting too close to the man, and pulled the door open.

"Lie down on your stomach."

The guy did as instructed and Taylor pulled another tie and bound the man's ankles, then ripped off a piece of the mans shirt and used it to repeat the washcloth trick, tying the man's mouth shut and then pushing him further into the seat, closing it on him. The back seat had a steel mesh partition separating it from the front, and the doors had no interior handles.

It wouldn't be a comfortable evening for him, but he'd be okay until the cavalry arrived.

Once the guy was secure, he moved back to the front, grabbed the radio, the gun, and the keys from the passenger seat.

He'd heard the radio going off as he was securing the deputy. It crackled to life again a few seconds after he picked it up, the voice on the other end getting testy.

"Unit Three, get off your damn phone and give me your status."

Maybe the deputy had learned his lesson about that now, since not paying attention led to him being trussed up like a hog in his own back seat with a washcloth jammed in his mouth.

Taylor pressed the transmit button and, using the best imitation he could muster, he said, "No visual yet."

There was a pause, and then the voice on the radio said, "Copy that."

Taylor went to the trunk and tossed the radio and the gun in it before slamming it shut and going around to the driver's side.

He backed the car out of the turnout and drove down until he was at the outskirts of the town, just where the trees thinned. Pulling onto a side road and in front of some kind of industrial building that looked empty, he shut the car off, locked it, and pocketed the keys.

Someone might come around and find the deputy, but it would be hell to get him out, and Taylor would be in the station before that happened.

He was going to walk the rest of the way. He moved between buildings and what cover there was, parallel to the road but staying off the pavement as much as he could, in case anyone else was out there looking for him.

Fifteen minutes later, he was looking at the courthouse that he'd walked into for the first time just a few days before.

The sheriff's office sat on the west side of the courthouse square, attached to the main building like an afterthought. The courthouse itself was three stories of Classical Revival brick and limestone, the kind every small Midwest town built to feel like old America. The sheriff's office was a smaller two-story brick structure extending from the left side of the courthouse, with SHERIFF in bold letters above the glass doors at the front.

Taylor circled, approaching from the south, staying in the shadows between buildings. He reached the rear of the sheriff's office and crouched behind a dumpster. The building had two back corners, one where it connected to the courthouse, and one that stood alone. A narrow alley separated the sheriff's office from a two-story concrete block building fifty feet to the south. A covered walkway connected the two structures halfway down the alley, elevated six feet off the ground with steel steps leading up on both ends.

Taylor moved closer. The sheriff's office had a rear door, solid steel with a small wire-reinforced window at eye level. The covered walkway had doors at both ends, same construction, same wire-reinforced glass.

He studied the layout. If Brody had Julia and Milly in the jail, that walkway was the most direct route between the two buildings. The jail's front entrance faced east, toward a side street off the square, but the walkway offered a second path.

Taylor checked his watch. 10:26 p.m. Fourteen minutes until Brody's deadline.

He wasn't going through the front door.

Chapter 14

Taylor stood in the shadows in the alley with his back pressed against the rough brick of the sheriff's station wall. It had taken too long to get here. He was five minutes past his deadline, and he was sure Brody had called him again to make threats.

Not that he would know. This close, he'd already shut off his phone to keep it from giving him away.

Besides, right now, Brody should be in a panic, trying to figure out what to do. Sure, he could hurt the women, but that wouldn't help him. Taylor had Hutchins, and Hutchins could doom him if he talked. For all he knew, Taylor was ruthless enough to leave the women to their own fate and take Hutchins straight to state or federal agencies to spill his guts.

Brody would be pacing, sweating, and looking at his phone every few seconds, wondering what Taylor was doing. He'd want to know why his guys hadn't called in. He might have even tried one and found he wasn't answering, panicking him more.

He would be imagining scenarios, working himself up. Taylor hoped so. Fear made men stupid, slow, and prone to mistakes.

Of course, it also made them dangerous. If he waited too long, Brody would panic and do something truly stupid. Something Taylor couldn't allow to happen.

The door was too thick to hear through and probably led into the cell block.

Or at least, he hoped so.

He had the deputy's keyring, which had four keys on it, plus the fob to the cruiser. Two were standard Yale keys, likely for the ignition and a locker; one was a square-headed brass key, probably for the station's front door or an interior office; and one was a Medeco.

It had steeply angled cuts and was thicker than the standard key, the kind of key for a high-security door you'd find on the outside of a jailhouse.

Taylor edged up next to the door and peeked through the corner of the wire-mesh glass. His view was limited, but he could see a pale green sally port corridor, the far end of which held a booking desk behind a partition.

Sitting at the desk was a deputy. Thick-necked, young-looking, wearing the tan uniform of the county sheriff's department. He was leaning back in a swivel chair, boots up on the desk, reading a magazine and facing away from the door.

No panic or nervousness. For him, it was just another night of jail duty, which meant he probably didn't know about the scheme with Hutchins and that tonight wasn't just another night.

Taylor ducked back down.

Transferring his pistol to his other hand, he took the Medeco key between his thumb and forefinger and clamped the other keys tight against his palm to keep them from jingling before inserting it into the deadbolt.

It went in smoothly. He applied pressure and found the mechanism stiff, which he'd expected, and kept turning the key, slowly and steadily, trying to reduce the noise as much as possible until the bolt retracted with a heavy thunk.

Taylor turned the handle and opened the door about three inches, peeking in and ready to move if he'd alerted the guard.

The deputy hadn't moved. Taylor couldn't hear it from outside the door, but a small radio was playing top forty greatest hits, which mixed with the ambient hum of the building's HVAC and the other noises of an older building like this.

Taylor opened the door wider, slipped inside, and eased it shut behind him, not bothering to re-engage the deadbolt. He might need to leave in a hurry.

Taylor moved down the corridor, staying close to the wall.

When the deputy was thirty feet away, still absorbed in his magazine, Taylor closed the distance. Even at ten feet, the man didn't seem to hear or suspect anything.

Zero situational awareness.

At five feet, Taylor froze as the man let out a long sigh and shifted forward, but it was only to reach for a Styrofoam cup on the desk, which he picked up and took a sip from, making a face before setting it back down.

Taylor was being careful. All the guy had to do was scream, and things would get a lot harder.

He was close enough now, though. He closed the last five feet in a rush, reversing his pistol in his hand, gripping the polymer frame and using the heavy steel slide as a hammer, bringing it down hard on the base of the deputy's skull, just behind the ear. It was a precise target.

If he brought it too low, he'd damage the spine, and too high, it would only hurt without taking the guy out. He had to hit that sweet spot right where the vagus nerve was.

The resulting sound was a dull, wet thud.

The deputy's head snapped forward, his body going limp as the magazine slipped from his fingers and fluttered to the floor.

Taylor reached out quickly as the guy slumped sideways and started to slide out of his chair, keeping him from smashing onto the floor and making too much noise.

When he caught him, the guy was dead weight, maybe two hundred pounds or a little more. Taylor took the strain in his legs, lowering the unconscious man gently to the linoleum.

He stopped to listen. The action hadn't been loud, but it hadn't been silent either.

No shouts or running feet. He was still good.

Taylor checked the man's pulse, which was strong and steady. He was out cold, and he would stay that way for a little bit. He'd also have a hell of a headache for a week.

Unfortunately, Taylor had run light on zip ties; he only had one left.

Taylor stripped the man's belt, taking the handcuffs from the case at the back before rolling the deputy onto his stomach and pulling his arms behind his back, and ratcheting the cuffs tight. He took a roll of duct tape from the booking desk, there was always duct tape, and wrapped a section around the man's head, covering his mouth but not his nose. He then took his last zip tie and pulled the man's feet together, cinching it closed.

That guy wasn't going anywhere.

He rifled the deputy's pockets and found a small set of personal car keys with the set of jail keys on a retractable belt clip.

Taylor took them both before looking around the booking area again. To his left, a heavy steel door led to the cell block. To his right, a hallway led toward the front of the building, toward the sheriff's offices and the courthouse connection.

He went left.

The steel door was locked. He tried three keys before he found the right one and pushed the door open.

The cell block was older than the rest of the building. The walls were painted concrete block, chipped in places to reveal older layers of institutional green and cream. There were six cells, three on each side of a central corridor. The fronts were barred, floor to ceiling. No privacy. No dignity.

Only two cells were occupied.

On the left, in the middle cell, a woman sat on the cot wearing a blouse and slacks, now wrinkled and stained, and her hair was disheveled. Her knees were pulled up to her chest, and she looked up as the door opened, her eyes wide, ringed with red.

He didn't know her, but he had to assume it was Julia Henley, because the right cell held Milly, who was pacing back and forth, looking furious as he came in.

She stopped and opened her mouth like she was going to complain or yell, but she stopped cold as she recognized him.

"Taylor!" Milly said.

"Shh," Taylor whispered, making a shushing gesture as she approached him.

He stopped between the two cells.

"Who is he?" Julia asked. Her voice was thin, trembling. "Is he with them?"

"He's the cavalry," Milly said. "Took you long enough."

"Sorry, I hit traffic," Taylor said as he sorted through the keys.

It took him a second, but he found the right keys and opened the two cells as quietly as he could, freeing both women.

Julia didn't move, just stared at him as if it were some kind of trick.

"Come on," Taylor said. "We don't have much time."

"My husband?" she asked as Milly joined them. "They said they were going to hurt him."

"He's safe. He's with a friend of mine, and it will be a while before they find him. This'll all be over by then."

She sagged, the tension leaving her body so fast she almost fell. Taylor steadied her with a hand on her shoulder.

"Where's Brody?" she asked.

"That was going to be my question. Do you know how many men he has with him?"

"Two that I saw. Tiller and Collins, his two buddies. The rest I saw take off just as I was being brought in here, except Frank there."

"We need to move," Taylor said, handing Milly the car keys he'd taken from the guy he assumed was Frank. "Listen to me carefully. You're going out the back door. It's open, and the alley is clear. Move fast, stay in the shadows, and go around the north side of the courthouse to the parking lot."

"Then what?" Milly asked.

"Find out what car these keys belong to and hit the panic button. I'm going to need a distraction. Once the alarm goes off, I want you to run. Go around to the other side of the courthouse. I saw a basement entrance on the east side, under the steps. It's probably locked, but there's a little dip you can duck into and be out of sight. Brody has those other guys out there, and I don't know how many of them are in on all this, so hide there and wait until I clear this up or the real cavalry gets here. Feds and probably state cops are already on their way and should be here soon. I hope."

"What are you going to do?" Julia asked.

"I'm going to finish this," Taylor said.

"They'll kill you," she said.

"They'll certainly try," he said, before turning to Milly. "Can you handle her?"

Milly grabbed Julia's hand. "I've got her. Don't worry about us."

"Go," Taylor said. "Give me two minutes to get into position, then hit that button."

Milly squeezed his arm. "Be careful, John."

"Go."

They all left the cell area, and Taylor watched them turn and hurry down the corridor, stepping over Frank, with Julia giving him a sad look before disappearing out the heavy back door.

He moved to the hallway that led to the front. The architecture changed here, with the concrete block giving way to drywall and wood paneling. The floor switched from linoleum to commercial carpet, the low-pile gray kind favored by poor municipalities.

The hallway was thirty feet long and ended in a T-junction. Taylor had been here once before, when Brody had tried to arrest him, and he remembered the layout. To the left was what looked like a break room and the evidence locker, and to the right was the bullpen with the main area, desks, and a doorway to the front lobby.

Taylor moved down the hall, his weapon low and close to his body, stopping when he reached the corner and listened. He could hear them, and he was right.

They were panicking.

"He's not coming," a voice said. Collins, Taylor thought. "It's been twenty minutes, Sheriff, he's playing us."

"Shut up," Brody said. "He'll have to come. I read about him; he won't leave the women."

"Maybe he called the Feds," Tiller said. "Maybe they're setting up a perimeter right now."

"Don't be an idiot. We'd know," Brody said. "We'd see the lights."

"I don't like it," Collins said. "I'm going to check the back."

"You're not going anywhere. You're staying on your side of the door. I want you both in place when he comes through it. He's that kind of guy. Arrogant as hell, thinks he's John Wayne."

Taylor smiled in the darkness. He wasn't John Wayne. John Wayne was an actor. John Wayne used blanks.

Taylor waited, counting the seconds in his head.

One Mississippi. Two Mississippi.

He visualized the layout of the bullpen, pulling up the memory from a few days ago. A large open room, four desks arranged in a square in the center, and a counter separating the public waiting area from the squad room. Brody's office in the back corner, glass-walled with the blinds drawn.

The desks were particle board and wouldn't stop a bullet. The counter was better, plywood and laminate, maybe a steel kickplate. The file cabinets along the wall were the only hard cover.

Forty-five Mississippi. Forty-six.

"I'm telling you, something feels wrong," Collins said.

"Stop whining and keep your eyes on the glass."

Fifty-eight. Fifty-nine. Sixty.

Two minutes.

HONK. HONK. HONK. HONK.

After the silence outside the courthouse and how on edge everyone inside was, the car alarm sounded like an air raid siren.

"What the hell?" Tiller yelled.

"He's here!" Collins shouted. "Out in the lot!"

"He's flanking us!" Brody screamed. "Move! Get to the back!"

Boots thudded on the carpet. Commotion. Confusion. The sound of furniture bumping.

Taylor stepped around the corner.

He didn't run. Running would make it harder to aim. He walked, taking each step smooth and steady, holding his weapon up and already aiming as he entered the bullpen.

The scene was chaotic.

Deputy Collins was near the front door, spinning around, his shotgun raised, looking toward the noise outside. Deputy Tiller was scrambling away from the side window, moving toward the hallway where Taylor now stood.

Sheriff Brody was standing by his office door, a heavy revolver in his hand, his head turned toward the back wall.

They were looking the wrong way, toward the sound of the noise in the parking lot.

It's a biological imperative. The brain prioritizes sudden, loud sounds and forces the eyes to turn, overriding training.

Not that these guys had much training.

Taylor acquired the first target, Tiller, who was several steps closer and was moving toward Taylor, his weapon coming up as his brain registered the new threat. Reacting way too late.

Taylor fired.

Crack-crack.

Two shots, a controlled pair, hit Tiller first in the upper chest, just below the throat and above where a vest would stop, punching in through bone and maybe into the spine. Not that it would matter, since the second hit just below his eye.

The physics of the impacts stopped Tiller's forward momentum. He didn't fly backward; that only happens in movies, although his head did snap back as the bullet punched through his cheek and into his brain. His knees buckled and his gun dropped from his hand as he folded straight down, like a puppet with cut strings.

Taylor traversed right, toward Collins. The deputy at the front door had spun around, his pump-action shotgun, a Remington 870, started to follow through toward Taylor. It was a good weapon, devastating at close range, but slower to maneuver, and the deputy had been caught completely flat-footed.

Taylor didn't hesitate; he shifted his aim, pointing center mass and then a little up. Collins was bringing the shotgun up as Taylor fired.

Crack.

The bullet took Collins in the throat. It wasn't where Taylor had aimed; he had aimed for the top of the sternum again, since it was a larger target also not covered by the vest, but Collins had started to duck, flinching as he tried to bring the stock to his shoulder.

The result was the same.

Collins dropped the shotgun as his hands went for his neck. Blood sprayed between his fingers, bright arterial red as he stumbled and fell over backward, hitting the glass of the front door with a heavy thud, sliding down to the floor.

Two down in about four seconds.

Taylor kept moving. He advanced into the room, not stopping to admire his work, looking for his third target.

For Brody.

The sheriff had vanished. Taylor swung his weapon, sweeping across the room, looking for where the man could have gone.

A shot rang out.

BOOM.

The sound was from a heavy caliber. A .357 or a .44, the sound was deafening in the enclosed space.

A chunk of plaster exploded from the wall six inches from Taylor's head, showering him in plaster dust.

Taylor dropped, going to one knee behind the nearest desk.

"You son of a bitch!" Brody screamed.

The voice came from inside the glass-walled office.

Taylor assessed. The office had glass walls, but they had blinds, and he couldn't see Brody.

Of course, Brody couldn't see him either.

"Give it up, Brody!" Taylor said. "It's over."

"Go to hell!"

Two more shots. The bullets punched through the drywall partition of the office and slammed into the front of the desk next to the one Taylor was using for cover. The particle board splintered as the bullets passed through and buried themselves in the carpet.

The desk was concealment, not cover. It hid him, but it wouldn't stop a magnum round. Taylor needed to move.

He looked at the layout. Brody was in the office. One door. One window looking out over the bullpen. The blinds were closed, but the slats were bent where Brody was peeking through.

Taylor reached into his pocket. He pulled out the heavy brass key he had taken from the ring. He waited.

"My deputies are coming!"

"Your deputies are asleep," Taylor said. "Or dead."

"Liar!"

"Check the radio."

Silence.

Then he heard the sound of movement inside the office. A drawer opening. Brody was reloading, or getting a backup weapon.

Taylor moved.

He lunged from behind the desk, sprinting low and hard toward the file cabinets on the far wall. They were heavy-gauge steel. They might not stop those large caliber bullets, but they'd be better than the desk.

Brody fired blindly through the glass, and the window shattered, shards spraying across the bullpen floor. The blinds twisted and hung askew.

Taylor slid behind the file cabinets and got back on one knee, keeping low. He was fifteen feet from the office door.

"You're done, Brody. Hutchins is in custody, the Doc flipped on you, and I have his files. I have the toxicology reports and everything else the Doc was keeping as an insurance policy. It's over."

"I am the law in this town!" Brody shouted.

His voice was cracking now. Panic was setting in.

"Not anymore."

Taylor listened. The man was breathing hard. He needed to flush Brody out. Taylor looked around. On top of the file cabinet was a heavy glass jar filled with peppermint candies, probably put there by a receptionist and forgotten.

Taylor grabbed the jar and weighed it in his hand. About five pounds, heavy enough.

He pitched it hard and high, over the top of the partition, aiming for the far corner of the bullpen, away from his position. The jar hit the floor with a massive crash, shattering and sending candy scattering across the tile.

Brody reacted, firing wildly toward the sound.

He clipped part of the blinds and they half fell down, exposing a third of the office. Taylor could see Brody through it, the big revolver extended, looking completely panicked.

This was a man who'd never faced real violence where his life was actually at stake.

Taylor stepped out from behind the file cabinets. He didn't shout a warning or ask for surrender. Brody had made his choice when he pulled the trigger the first time.

Taylor raised the weapon in both hands and drew a bead.

Brody must have seen the movement because he started to turn, the revolver swinging back toward Taylor; his eyes were wide, bulging with adrenaline and rage. His mouth was open in a snarl.

He was way too slow. Taylor squeezed the trigger.

The bullet hit Brody in the shoulder, spinning him around, the revolver flying out of his hand. His arms had flown up and the second bullet went in just below the armpit, across and into his body, probably ripping through his lungs and maybe more.

Brody collapsed, hitting the floor hard, face down.

Taylor walked forward, his weapon still trained on the man as he came through the shattered glass door, kicking the revolver clear when he got to him, sending it sliding under Brody's desk.

The sheriff groaned and tried to push himself up, but his arms weren't working. He kind of rolled onto his back instead, looking up at Taylor. His face was gray and sweat beaded on his forehead.

"You ..." he gasped. "You can't ..."

"I just did," Taylor said.

"I'm ... the sheriff."

"You're a criminal. You killed Roy Breyer and five other people, all for money."

"It was business," he coughed out.

"It was murder."

Brody coughed again, blood flecking his lips. "You're going to jail, Taylor. You're a cop killer. They'll fry you."

"We'll see," Taylor said, looking down at Brody as he gasped twice, let out a wet gurgle, and died.

Chapter 15

An hour and a half later, the sheriff's station looked like a federal crime scene, which it was.

Taylor sat on the front steps of the courthouse, fifty feet from the station entrance. Yellow tape stretched across the front door of the station, and portable floodlights had been set up, turning night into day.

State police cruisers filled the lot along with three FBI Suburbans lined up in a row near the street.

Inside, through the shattered front door that had taken a bullet at some point in the shootout, he could see technicians working, swabbing blood splatter, photographing bodies, and processing the scene.

Julia Henley sat on a bench in front of the courthouse, visible but out of the way. A female state trooper sat with her. Thankfully, she'd stopped crying at some point in the last twenty minutes.

Not that Taylor blamed her. It was a lot to take in. Milly was sitting on a bench on the other side of the door from her, a lot less emotional. She was her father's daughter, after all, and was mostly just taking it all in.

Another SUV pulled into the lot with government plates, stopping near the tape line, and Whitaker got out.

She'd made good time since he'd called her after picking up Henley, what seemed like a lifetime ago instead of the four hours it had been.

She'd made amazing time and must have taken the FBI jet. It was probably worth it. Hutchins had taken in millions of taxpayer dollars and killed a government employee. This would be front-page news, and she'd probably end up on TV at some point.

Worth the price of a plane ticket.

Taylor pushed himself up off the steps as her eyes fell on him, and she started walking toward him, ducking under the police tape and showing her ID to the state trooper who'd moved to intercept her.

"At some point, you're going to have to learn what 'sit tight' means," she said, stopping in front of him.

"You're surprised?"

"Not even a little, but you left ten guys hog-tied across a five-mile area, including two cops, plus three more dead cops inside, and that doesn't even count the two dead from this afternoon. It's quite the mess to sort out."

"To be fair, they were crooked cops, and they were shooting at me."

"Which is why you aren't in cuffs. Actually, as shootouts go, it's pretty clean. Between what the women will tell us and what I'm sure we'll get from Hutchins and Henley, it'll be pretty clear you were operating to save lives, although this would be easier if you were still working with the bureau."

"They could always take me back."

"Yeah? I don't see that happening."

"So you sent someone for Henley?"

"One of the troopers is up there now, and I have agents on the way to take Doctor Henley into protective custody and take him down to the field office. The trooper already confirmed he has a stack of evidence for us, so it shouldn't take much work to prove a criminal conspiracy. Hutchins will be going away for a long time."

"You probably need to go get him. I left him tied up."

"I know. They recovered him from the trunk of a Tahoe a few minutes after I touched down. He's got a nasty concussion and some broken bones, so he'll be in the hospital for a while, but he's already under arrest, and he isn't going anywhere. His operation is finished."

"The town along with it, probably."

"Probably. I gathered this was their last lifeline. For now, the state police will take over law enforcement in Glacier Falls until we sort out which of the remaining deputies were involved, but that'll take some time. There will be hearings, indictments, trials. It'll take months to unravel."

"I figured. At least Roy gets some justice."

"There is that. You ready to get out of here?"

"Yeah. Let me go say goodbye to Milly first," Taylor said, starting toward the courthouse, Whitaker following behind.

Milly looked up as he approached.

"Hey," she said.

"Hey."

"What happens now?" she asked.

"The FBI processes the case, and Hutchins goes to jail for years. There will have to be a cleanup, and the groundwater around here will be a mess for a while. Who knows how long the town will keep going."

"I couldn't care less," she said. "It isn't my town, and they killed my father. The whole place can burn."

"Fair enough. Are you going to arrange a funeral for him, now that you can get his body and it's all over?"

"Yeah. I'll call the Department of Defense. He rates a military funeral, and after all this, I think he should get it."

"God, he'd hate that."

"I know," she said, smiling. "What about you?"

"Back to DC and my girls, I guess."

"I'm glad. I always thought you'd make a good dad."

"You were the only one," Taylor said.

"Goodbye, Taylor," she said, reaching out and squeezing his arm.

He patted her hand and walked away. She knew him well enough to know he didn't love goodbyes. He headed back to the SUV with Whitaker in tow.

"Okay, let's get back home. I need a shower and some sleep," he said, climbing in.

The End

About the author

Travis writes science fiction, fantasy, and thriller novels (and the occasional coming-of-age story), with the hope of transporting and enthralling readers. Publishing novels since 2015, Travis's passion is creating worlds and characters that live and breathe, and experiencing the joy of those stories with his readers. When not writing, Travis enjoys connecting with readers and other writers, managing the popular Complete Marvel Reading Order website, where he works on his other passion for comics and graphic novels, and spending time with his family. If you have enjoyed this book, please consider taking a moment to rate or review it wherever you found your copy, as it helps new readers find my works and ensures I can continue writing book into the future.

Find out more at:
amazon.com/TravisStarnes/e/B072YBDC3S/

Or visit
https://tstarnes.com

Signup to get free previews and notifications of upcoming books at
http://tstarnes.com/preview-notification-newsletter/

Also by

John Taylor Stories

Rebirth
False Signs
The Wrong Girl
Burying the Past
Family Ties
Election Day
Danger Close
Extraction
Designated Target
Border Crossed
Desperate Rendition
Broken Ground

Country Roads Series

Playing by Ear
Fanfare
Dissonance
Elegy
From the Top
Center Stage

Imperium Series

Volume 1
The Sword of Jupiter
The Trumpets of Mars
The Sands of Saturn
The Depths of Neptune
The Fires of Vulcan
The Triumph of Venus
Volume 2
The Wings of Mercury
The Plains of Pluto
The Clouds of Caelus
The Masks of Janus

Shattered Lands Series

In the Shadow of Lions
An Ending of Oaths
The Barons' War
Heavy Lies the Crown

False Start Series

Second Down
Scramble
Loss of Down

The Veilguard Saga

Threads of Destiny
The Blackstar Legacy

Stand Alone

Going Home

www.ingramcontent.com/pod-product-compliance
Lightning Source LLC
Chambersburg PA
CBHW061239170626
46809CB00007B/2747
9781960747389